In Search of the Lambs

and Other Stories

In Search of the Lambs

Lambs

and Other Stories

by

Divyank J.

Lighted Lake Press

For Jenny

Table of Contents

A Long March Home

The beam of a flashlight waved in the darkness and stopped as soon as it reached their faces. Omar and his nine-year-old son, Jamal, were confronted by a man in khaki. He had seen them coming from behind the barricades that blocked the road. Omar, gripping Jamal's hand, slowly came closer. The short policeman looked into Omar's deep, sunken eyes, inspected their travel-exhausted faces.

"Where are you coming from?" the policeman asked.

"Delhi," Omar hesitated for a moment before he answered. Without being asked, he began to scrabble about in his pockets for any piece of paper that would prove his identity.

"Where are you going?" He continued flashing light into their eyes.

Omar, in the agitation of not finding anything valuable in his pockets except a few rupee notes, looked around nervously. He stepped back.

"Where are you going?" the policeman demanded again, louder this time.

"Badeu!" Omar replied. He felt a little courage gathering inside his chest. "It's far from here, sahib, and we need to keep on walking."

"No, you cannot," said another man in a dry voice. He was sitting in a chair by the ambulance that stood parallel to the barricades with its side lights pulsing.

The yellow light coming from behind the man sitting sharpened the edges of his uniform. He had an upturned mustache, a sturdy physique, and the self-assured way he was seated—one leg carelessly placed on the knee of the other—distinguished him as some sort of senior to the short one. Omar dared not respond to him; instead, he looked down at his boy, who regarded him with a dubious expression.

After eyeing them from head to toe, the seated policeman knocked behind him on the ambulance door. Moments later a fat doctor stepped out of the ambulance, putting on his gloves.

"Cover up your damn mouths!" the senior policeman commanded Omar and his son.

The doctor, in a white PPE suit that covered his entire body except for his eyes, came over and put a weird pistol-like white machine against Omar's forehead and then Jamal's. The doctor's old, tiny eyes above the blueish N-95 mask examined Jamal suspiciously. Then he grabbed his skinny wrist in his gloved hand before he touched his forehead for inspection.

"He's got a fever," the doctor informed the policemen.

"Do you have a cough or a cold?" the doctor asked.

"No!" Omar answered.

"And any trouble in breathing, child?" the doctor asked directly to the boy, not his father.

"No, not at all," Omar answered instead, pressing his boy against his left thigh. "He's all right!"

However, Omar knew that the last weekend hadn't been very good for Jamal, as he had had a mild fever. And, before they set out for their town, he also had vomited a few times. But after they had begun their journey, he had not been sick even once. All along the way, he proved himself really to be a strong boy. Jamal walked slower than Omar had wanted, but he assured himself they were not in that much of a hurry.

Jamal didn't even talk about his mother. Every other time when Jamal had been afflicted with fever or something, he became gawky and blurted nonstop about his mother. But not this time. He walked beside Omar as they crossed cities and towns under the burning April sun. Jamal was healthy and strong like Omar used to be in his childhood. Always Omar saw his own personality in his child's behavior and was certain about Jamal's present condition.

He is NOT sick. At least he doesn't look sick standing here by me, letting the doctor inspect him with this confidence.

"Both of you must spend the night here," the first policeman told them.

"I can't...sahib," Omar protested politely, but then peering down into the eyes of the senior one, he realized he shouldn't have. A drop of cold sweat rolled down from his forehead and dripped onto his collarbone. He said, "Please sahib, let us go."

The men in khaki didn't answer.

"I beg you, sahib. We still have far to go," Omar urged, holding both his hands together.

The father and the son had already covered half the distance to their goal. How could they halt their journey in the middle? The chaos of the present day gave visions of an ultimate fate of a doomed humankind. Omar had been conditioned for such a long, long journey on foot and was sure that his son, being young, was just as fit.

JUST KEEP ON WALKING! If you stay in one place for a time more than necessary, you are finished right there. How in the world could we waste the whole night in a shelter?

"Listen, in the morning we'll arrange a bus for the people like you who stayed here in the shelter." The short policeman leaning over the barricades pointed at a big yellow bulb behind him, illuminating a portion of a footpath and the leaves of a ficus tree on the left. There was a huge tent behind. Omar moved his gaze back to the policeman's face that now expressed a little concern for their condition, especially for his boy. "And still, if you don't care about your sick son," the policeman said, taunting, "you can go. Yes, go!" He opened the barricades slightly, making a pretense of letting them go through.

"Are they all idiots?" The other policeman stood up from the chair, masked his face, came forward, and rebuked Omar, "The two hundred people who are waiting for the buses, are they all idiots? Do you even know what this disease is? You want to spread it and kill all of us, you dumb, nasty people?" His reddened eyes were disturbingly upset. Both men in khaki exchanged glances and the first one looked down.

"But sahib..." Omar tried to speak.

"Move to the shelter now, you scum!" The command of the senior policeman loudly ripped apart the thin night wind. He jerked the barricade shut before him. Thoroughly dejected now, Omar turned to the left and glared down at the barricade that stood between him and his hometown.

* * *

Nearly every inch of the shelter was already occupied, yet the whole night long people kept coming in with their crying children. They filled the entire tent with the scent of sweat and vomit as most of them were violently sick. For Omar, it was not strange that almost all the children were crying out of hunger, sudden stomach cramps, and seasonal ailments. Yet, his son remained silent throughout the night. Jamal was brave and strong and had proved himself on the journey by walking along with his tall, lean father. Omar knew they would eventually get through. This delay was only a matter of a night.

They found a spot to one side where people didn't seem so sick. Omar hoped this would be safe for Jamal. They spent the night in the shelter, not in the hope of an easy morning or for the bus that could reduce the unbearable distance, but because Omar knew more rest would be good for his son.

If he is getting sick again...if the doctor was right...if...no! No, he isn't. My boy is all right. Omar kept muttering to himself as he lay beside Jamal in the tent, put his hand on his own chest, and felt. He looked out beyond a loose triangle of the tent that flapped with the wind; the scattered clouds above were silently sailing exposing something that didn't change. He saw the stars and studied their usual patterns, at least for a moment everything seemed normal again.

He's not sick. He's all right.

In the morning, most of the migrant workers gathered outside the tent, waiting for the bus to take them away, somewhere, perhaps to their homes. They waited for two hours, and together, they witnessed the sun rising over distant farms, the only normal occurrence of the forthcoming day. Many of them, as hopeless as Omar, began to walk down the road by themselves.

"Everything will be all right, once you reach home. Jamal will be all right," Omar contented himself before picking up the bag.

"Can you walk?" he asked his son.

"Yes Abbu, I can," Jamal replied with a weary smile.

As they began to move out of the cool shadow of the ficus tree by the shelter, a white vehicle came from the opposite direction. It was not a passenger vehicle, which had been promised, and they all were hoping for, but a compact van. A white flag with red poppies as an emblem was waving on its top beside a loudspeaker.

"Food Packets!" The voice through the loudspeaker resounded in the fresh morning air, reminding them of everything that went rogue during the last few days and their now-uncertain future. "Food Packets! Come over here all of you. Stand in line."

The policemen weren't on this side of the tent. People rushed, bringing down the barricades. At the entreaties of the two young gentlemen who got out of the van wearing white *kurtas*. The people formed themselves into two queues even though hunger was forcing them to shatter the thin glass of social codes. Omar was happy to get two packets because he stood in the first row and his son in the second. Many families were given only one packet, and unfortunately, many were left empty-handed; they watched the van rush back to where it came from; it disappeared into the grayness of the road like their fleeting hopes.

Omar instructed his son to put the packets inside their bag as shrewdly as he could since hungry eyes were staring at their greedy hands. Omar knew they were hungry too. If it was a different day, he would have given away one of the packets, but sadly it wasn't a different day. It wasn't going to be a normal day and they, themselves, still had to go far, far away.

Omar and Jamal plodded along the National Highway 2 which connects Delhi to Bihar. Omar had always seen it filled with overloaded trucks and buses dominating the road; taxis coming or going rapidly;

dusty cars speeding up, overtaking each other, sometimes so swiftly you could not spot them passing by, and sometimes honking horns continuously. There might even be a mile-long traffic jam on some bad days. Today, as far as his eyes could see, the road was strangely and terrifyingly empty. Omar had seen severe wrecks, even fatal accidents, that had not scared him as much as this emptiness did. But they had to continue their journey embracing whatever came their way.

After traveling on the serpent-like road in a valley, they made a half-circle around a large lake and with it, comfortably, left five more towns behind. All looked just the same: gray and dusty under the sun as if even the dead had deserted them. However, they were not alone. Many pedestrians appeared. Some walked beside them as if they were companions and moved like a herd of animals; no one knew who was from what place. Walking shoulder to shoulder, they looked alike, as if they all were a part of that singular human fate that no one could escape. With bags on their shoulders, panting but walking, sweating like hell, they were hopeful they were going back to their home.

Omar and Jamal stopped many times, relaxed their aching legs in the cool water of ponds and rested with their backs against tree trunks, and stretched out in the shade.

"I can walk, Abbu," Jamal would assure his father after each short rest. "We have to go home. Just keep walking, remember?"

Omar had repeatedly touched Jamal's forehead to ensure that the doctor was wrong. And he was: Jamal no longer had a fever. To avoid direct sunlight, Omar poured some water from his plastic bottle to dampen his handkerchief so he could cover his son's head with it.

"I like it, Abbu," Jamal said.

They walked along the highway for a few hours, resting several times, then took a shorter route. They walked in the shadow of blue gum trees that grew on both sides of that narrow, cracked road.

"Look at the trees, Abbu. They are just like the trees at our farm, aren't they?"

Omar looked back at his son; beads of sweat shone on his forehead, and he walked with his shoulders bent low.

"It's a good place to eat," Omar suggested.

Under the rustling leaves of gum trees, they gobbled down the food which they had been carrying since morning. Shortly after eating, Jamal vomited everything out over his rugged trousers and cracked shoes. His face turned terribly red as he stood upright to look at his perplexed father.

Omar washed his son's clothes and his shoes in a stream and laid his son down on the meadow under a tree, and asked him to close his eyes for a while.

"You just need more rest, my boy." Omar, too, lay down, and glared at the splitted sun through the leaves of the gum trees, while the branches above were moving swiftly with the wind.

Jamal was right. Such trees were on all sides of our farm when... when we had the farm. Omar's father had planted many of them and Omar himself had watered them, and witnessed them getting taller just like he saw Jamal growing up.

On one bad day, those trees were gone and the farm was gone. Then Omar and his father were forced to leave the peace of their town behind. Darker thoughts invaded Omar's mind as the scary faces of the mustached policeman and the fat masked doctor at the barricade floated in front of his eyes. He couldn't see trees and the sky beyond them anymore.

Did I make the right choice? Shouldn't I have stayed in the city? Staying or leaving, that was not only his subjective state of confusion but the biggest question of the decade; a never-ending dilemma: to choose one of them as each came with its own grave consequences.

It's choosing that's always been difficult for me. But, it's much easier to lay down here in the cool shadow than to stay in the middle of the madness of the city. I made the right choice. Once we reach home, everything will be fine. Jamal will be fine.

He gave his most optimistic smile when Jamal woke up and his eyes looked for his father.

"Are you fine now?" the father asked.

"I think, yes, Abbu."

Although it was a dull answer, Jamal looked much better. It was the heat of the sun that made him vomit. All he needed was just a little more rest, and now he was ready to proceed on their long march home.

Omar trudged, and Jamal followed. They crossed three bridges that connected four towns, and saw the water under the bridges flowing uninterrupted. After they had passed two more towns, they waded through the shallow water of a river to take a shortcut to the next town. Then, Omar carried Jamal on his shoulders. Jamal's dirty shoes slapped back and forth on Omar's chest, painting their journey on his once-white shirt.

* * *

"I like this kind of road so much, why don't you make such roads, Abbu?" Jamal asked. He was aware of the kind of work his father used to do in the city. Omar didn't keep it a secret and was not ashamed of providing his cheap labor for road and gutter construction.

"All roads are alike, the only difference here are trees on both sides."

"But there are many trees in my school too and I don't like it."

"I thought you liked it."

"Never."

"So, what do you like then?"

"Our farm," Jamal answered wistfully. "Will we go there once we reach the town?"

"Yes, we'll go there too," Omar lied to his son.

"And then, we'll come back to the city, won't we?"

"I have no idea!" Omar looked away, so his son would not see into his eyes.

They walked on silently for some time.

"I know you'll go back to the city when the crisis is all over," Jamal said dismally, when both of them sat down on the side of a creek to cool down their legs in its water. The sun had descended a little but it was still hot. By now, Omar had acquired many cuts on his feet throughout the journey, and his thigh muscles ached. He cupped his hand and poured the cool water from the creek onto his legs continuously, which relaxed his whole body.

"Abbu, will you have to take me back to the city, later, with you?" Jamal asked. He looked worried.

"You don't want to live with me after all this ends?"

"No, I never wanted to," Jamal said bitterly. "You took me there."

"You don't like the city?" asked Omar. "Wasn't it a wonderful place with so many sky-touching buildings?"

"No, it was very bad, bad, bad. I like farms, the country, not buildings. And also I don't have even one friend there."

"You'll have many if you know how to make friends," said Omar, remembering his lonely past.

"I know one thing, I hate them... all of them. Why did you take me to the city, Abbu? It was all good when I was in our town, with Ammi."

"Okay! We won't go back if you stop talking about your Ammi."

"You're lying." Jamal stood up. "I have to go home... to my Ammi."

"Listen, Jamal," Omar held his son's skinny wrist, pulled him close, and touched his forehead; it was hot again. "Ammi no longer lives with us, I've told you many times," Omar said, brushing Jamal's frizzy hair away from his suntanned forehead.

"You're lying." Jamal released his hand from the grip of his father and started walking by himself. He didn't stop at his father's call even though he had started panting. "We must be walking. I have to go back to Ammi," Jamal insisted.

"I am not lying," Omar stood up, lifted their bag, and followed his son. "If you stop talking about your Ammi, we won't go back to the city. I promise."

"I wanted to live with her. You didn't care," cried Jamal and kicked a pebble in anger out of sight. "I don't get it. Why did we go to the city at all? We were so happy at our home, in our town." Jamal stopped, stamped his shoe, and turned to his father sobbing.

"We'll sit down here for a while, Son." Omar tried to take things under his control.

"I don't want to."

"See! You like such beautiful places, don't you?" Omar pointed towards the trees and a half-dried river flowing beyond the trees. In the water, boulders were half green with moss and half white under the sun. "Don't you like this all?"

"I've got a headache."

Omar made him sit on a flat rock by him in the shade of a tree.

"You sleep here in my lap."

"I just want to go home."

"My boy, don't think about it." Omar put his arm around his bony shoulders. "We'll soon be at our home," he assured him, kissing his sweaty forehead.

"Then why are we wasting our time?"

"Next to that hill, is our town," Omar pointed. "We're almost home. You can sleep in my lap now."

Instead of taking the road around the hill, Omar decided to climb it, taking an old trail. Omar carried his son who soon fell asleep. In the silence of the wilderness, Omar heard dead leaves being crushed under his worn-out shoes, and some old but malicious thoughts churned in his mind. Never could he gain control over those thoughts, no matter how hard he tried. Omar thought about the village; about the city and then about the catastrophe that had kicked them out of the city. Long ago, he had lost everything in the village and now, he had lost everything he left behind in the city. He knew that from the moment he had started this journey. Further questions about it would make no difference. Gone were those days when Jamal and his Ammi used to greet him with shy kisses and warm hugs. His son's toddler smile had gradually lost the magic of healing he had hoped for by relocating to the city. Sometimes, Omar wondered if he himself had snatched everything away from Jamal.

Who else is responsible for this destructive condition of his son? Who else is here to blame? His Ammi? She cannot be. It was me! It was me and only me.

When it was almost dark Omar reached the last part of the hill which was now almost dried out in the summer. The faint moonlight helped him recall the forgotten trail. As it grew steeper, he stopped to catch his breath and continued his march. The journey was about to end. He smiled. Before reaching the crest, he heard some faint rattling noise coming from the other side of the hill. The sound became louder and louder with his every step. Curious to know what was going on, he climbed faster.

Omar stood at the hilltop, breathing heavily from the climb as the wind blew his hair. He gazed down at his town. There were many beams of light waving all across the sky; to and fro, held by ecstatic hands. Victorious shouting merged with the deafening noise of cymbals and steel plates clanging and bells that resonated through the entire town and beyond.

What is going on here? Omar wondered, then realized: *They must be celebrating the end of the crisis!*

In this moment of astonishment, he patted his son's cheek to wake him up, to have a look at that exceptional view.

"Jamal!" he called. "This is magnificent! Look how beautiful our home is."

But Jamal didn't move. Omar looked down at his son's face. Jamal's head was loosely resting on his shoulder, his saliva had dribbled down his chin and onto Omar's shirt. His trembling hand touched his son's forehead; all the hotness had gone. It was now staggeringly cold. There was no breathing, no movement. Omar shook his son, but only his head rolled down from his shoulder.

"Jamal?" he shouted at the top of his lungs.

Caught up again by feelings of dread, Omar laid his son down on the uneven ground. His hands rushed frantically to search his son's skinny body to find a hint of life. Everywhere his frightened fingers touched, was cold and numb!

"Wake up, Jamal," Omar patted on his right cheek and then he gently slapped both his cheeks. "Jamal, we are home. Look! Look there... Your Ammi. She is here, coming for you with hundreds of flashlights in her hands. Yes, there she is," he said while his eyes searched Jamal for the slightest clue of any movement. But there was none.

"Please, wake up my boy!"

The cold, nine-year-old body didn't respond.

Omar, gasping for air, fell on the ground hopelessly. Tears rolled down his cheeks. Even though his heart pounded loudly in his ears, he could hear the thunderous music of bells, cymbals, gongs, and steel plates and the cries of hundreds of people. Above his head, light beams crossed each other as if searching for something in the sky; something that had just gone up there, beyond the clouds, beyond the moon, beyond the stars, and beyond everything he could see with his blurry eyes.

"My boy was strong..." Omar beat his fists on the ground. He fell down next to his son as he felt an immense pressure right in the center of his chest, breaking something into pieces, jumping from his chest to his throat and arms. He choked. His body jerked, then lay still.

The Pigeons

Saurabh shut the book down on the tea table. He was surprised to see the hands of the clock were still marking 5:40 p.m. He let out a sigh. Time dragged along like a sloth. He got up from the couch, stretched his fingers, yawned, then strolled leisurely across the hall for a few minutes before he moved to the balcony, in the back of his apartment.

The view from his balcony couldn't be considered a great view. Down below was a narrow street, a very narrow street, an alley really. It was too narrow for most vehicles. Opposite stood an old building. Standing there, all Saurabh could see was a huge, damp wall that had turned yellow over time with plaster peeling away in places. There was a window right across from his balcony which was always closed, but strangely today, it was wide open. An old man with copper-rimmed glasses and a cabbie cap was leaning out on his elbows, staring down at the empty street.

Despite being in different buildings, the men were so close to each other that it seemed that if Saurabh leaned a little, they could easily shake hands.

"Good evening, sir," said Saurabh, attempting to initiate conversation. He was bored of the slow passage of time and the novel which was about the fall of a family with a dull plot. He had been reading since morning and only read a quarter of the pages.

"Evening." The old man looked up and replied in a voice that hardly came out of his throat. His suntanned face was crisscrossed with uncountable wrinkles. Then he dropped his head low to peep into the right side of the street, not showing any interest in Saurabh.

"Are you waiting for the food van, sir?" Saurabh asked him after a pause.

"No," the old man said, then cleared his throat and spat. "Just taking in some fresh air."

Saurabh laughed. He took it as a rather sarcastic statement in contrast to the adverse situation they were collectively facing as a nation and a race. The news channels claimed the last time something like this happened it was called the "Black Death," in fourteenth-century Europe.

"I don't think the air is fresh anymore," Saurabh told the old man.

"What you think doesn't matter," the old man said cynically. "Look at them!" He pointed with his shaking finger at the pigeons perched one by one on the electric wires. "They don't care."

Saurabh, instead, looked down and shifted his gaze from right to left and then back again. The narrow street was covered with thousands of dead mango and neem leaves. And there were old stray dogs yawning while sitting on the top of dusty vehicles parked down there. Once too noisy, now the street was so silent that Saurabh could even hear the clock ticking behind him in the living room.

"Never in the last six years have I seen this road like this," Saurabh said dismally as he was somewhat annoyed by the silence and the emptiness. For as long as he could remember, the street had always been occupied with scooters honking horns, children running behind sugar candy sellers, and people hooting and selling fruits and vegetables on their pushcarts. It was irritating sometimes, but now he could say it all had kept the street alive.

"I haven't seen this many pigeons here together in the last twenty years," the old man said.

"You've been living here for twenty years?" Saurabh asked, observing the man's face. Certainly, he had never seen that old face before in this neighborhood. But then, he realized he had never truly paid attention to any of his neighbors. It was just the complete absence of work and the resulting boredom that drove him into this seemingly one-sided talk.

"Of course I live here, child. I am old. I have been old for the past twenty years. Where do you want me to go at this age?"

"I didn't mean that. I wonder if you live here by yourself."

"Yeah. A man of eighty-two can easily live on his own." After an awkward pause, the old man continued. "I am an artist, and an artist must live alone, regardless of what others feel about it." A long-lost sense of pride came back and his face seemed to glow for a moment as he declared himself an *artist*.

"Great! What do you paint, sir?" Saurabh grinned.

"I may look so boring to you, but I have made some amusing paintings."

"Are you working on something interesting right now?"

"I painted my last piece seven years ago before my wife died."

"Oh, I am so sorry. I'd love to see your collection someday. I appreciate good paintings."

"I'll show you something when I am ready. The younger generation doesn't like to wait, but pardon me, child, these pigeons never really come here over and over again."

Saurabh considered the pigeons for a moment. Sitting there, they too looked bored of their own monotonous life.

Does having wings make any difference at all? Saurabh wondered. As he looked at them, a few spread out their wings to fly. The sudden flutter of their wings jerked the wires and the rest of the birds, holding onto the wires, swung together up and down. As some more commenced to fly, the old man held his hand above his eyes and looked up in the sky where the pigeons were going. They collectively made a huge circle in the clear sky and disappeared behind a distant building. The old eyes became upset when they couldn't see them anymore.

"In case you're waiting for the van," Saurabh said after a short uncomfortable pause. "I must tell you, it comes at six o'clock. Do you need anything, sir?"

"No. Yesterday I got all the stuff I needed... for the whole two weeks... I need nothing now." The old man proudly smiled but didn't look into Saurabh's eyes. "Thank you for asking, though."

They both stood there, Saurabh looking down at the street and the old man staring at the remaining pigeons. Saurabh took out a packet of cigarettes from his pajamas. The old man observed him when he lit a cigarette, then looked back inside his darkened room.

"Does the van bring this too?" the old man asked.

"No, sir. The van only brings packaged food, milk, and groceries. But I have a stock. I don't know why. Maybe I've been collecting them for such an opportunity," he laughed ironically.

The old man didn't laugh at his joke but looked with longing at the cigarette pressed between Saurabh's lips.

"You can have one if you want. Take it, sir." Saurabh offered.

"Oh, no, child...I don't usually... oh, okay... just one. Give me one if you are forcing me."

Saurabh threw a cigarette across the space, then the lighter. The old man failed to catch both, but he picked them up off the floor. It took him a while to light the cigarette, then he tossed the lighter back and Saurabh grabbed it.

"What do you do?" the old man asked, after blowing the smoke out into the air.

"A software engineer," Saurabh said. as he also blew smoke out of his mouth.

"Oh. That's sad."

"It's sad, yes. That's why I'm sitting here at home. The company promised to pay half our salary, but I've received nothing in the last five months. Thanks to my father who taught me the necessity of saving money at a very early age, I had some saved. But it's not all about money. I want to work. Staying home for the whole day drives a man crazy. I think I should have been a doctor. They are the only ones busy now."

"A noble thought," the old man said. "They are really busy nowadays. I read it in the newspaper a few days ago."

"While studying, I dreamt of becoming a doctor and moving out of the country," Saurabh reflected. "Maybe even going to the USA someday like many other Indian doctors. Now I think it was a stupid idea."

"Why?"

"Don't you watch the news, sir? The situation seems out of control there."

"Worse than here?"

"Yeah, much worse. Just like hell."

"And, in Atlanta?" The old man was anxious as he pronounced *Atlanta* and stared into Saurabh's eyes as if searching for a genuine answer. He had forgotten about everything, even about the pigeons.

"Worse!"

"Oh, someone of mine lives there." The old man shook his head.

"May I ask who?" Saurabh asked.

The old man said nothing, only took a puff and slowly released the smoke from between his parched lips. His fingers, holding the cigarette tightly, were shivering. But his eyes were calm now. One could say, it made him feel good to watch the smoke go up in the sky where the pigeons had gone, as if he was flying around them.

"You live alone here, child?" the old man asked.

"Ah... yes. I do. A young man can also live on his own."

"Ha-ha. Are you married?"

"I was once."

"Any children?"

"Thankfully no."

"Where do your parents live?"

"That's a difficult question. My mother died when I was a baby."

"I'm sorry for that, and what about your father?"

"Sadly, he also passed away a few years ago. From a heart attack."

"I am so sorry. I thought otherwise..."

"It's okay. Had he been alive, I wouldn't leave him alone but would keep him here with me. He was the best father in the world."

"But you couldn't smoke like this in front of him. I never let my sons smoke or drink as long as I was in the house." The old man mocked and gave a clever smile. "Do you ever think of him?" he asked Saurabh as if taunting.

"What?"

"Don't you miss your father?"

"You have to forget things and move on."

"Right, child. Forgetting and moving on...yes...we all do that. You wouldn't believe it, I've almost forgotten my father's face, except for his thick eyebrows and trimmed beard." He threw the cigarette butt out as far as he could with all the strength left in his eighty-two-year-old hand. "Once," he continued, without matching eyes with Saurabh, "when I was young, and my mother wasn't home for some reason, my father taught me how to cook a delicious omelet. That's all he knew to cook in order to feed both of us. I've never forgotten his lessons. He was indeed a good teacher."

"My dad was different," Saurabh said as he took the last puff and let the butt slip from the grip of his fingers and watched it fall down to the street. "He always wanted me to settle down in a city and become something... something big. I don't know what he meant by "big." Then one day I received a call that..."

"Every father in this world thinks the same," the old man said and took off his glasses and wiped them clean on his chest. After putting them back on, he continued, "Forgetting the past... moving on. But I chose to stay close to my father till his last breath. I quit my job. You know what his last words were? 'It's a great feeling when you die in your son's lap.' That's what he said."

Saurabh couldn't take his eyes off the old man's face as complex emotions crossed it. Of course, the old man was hiding an ancient pain behind his worn-out skin, but there was more, something horrible. Saurabh shifted his gaze to the right; now there were more people peeping out of their balconies and windows.

"I don't think the van will come today," guessed Saurabh.

"Probably not," the old man agreed. He looked at the pigeons. The last of them began to fly away, except for one, a big, round pigeon that seemed too old to fly immediately. The old man moved uneasily and settled in his previous position.

"I don't want to embarrass you by asking over and over," Saurabh said. "But as you know, it is really a hard time for us, for our country, and for the entire world. In this time of crisis, we must help one another."

"That makes you a good human."

"Right, sir. So, do you need anything?" Saurabh asked, then waited for his reply.

"As I told you..." The old man looked back into his room, then down at his foot, and turned his head up. The copper rim of his glasses shone in the evening sun. "I bought all the stuff I needed yesterday." He looked down at his nervous hands and then up at the lone pigeon. "I got everything, but eggs. You just reminded me of my father, and I wish I could cook some eggs today. Do you... do you have any eggs?"

Saurabh smiled and immediately went inside and brought out a whole tray of eggs, then leaned as far as he could over the railing to hand it to the old man.

"Thank you." The proud old man tried hard not to make eye contact with him when he took the tray from the outstretched hand.

"Welcome," Saurabh said. "You can call me anytime if you need something."

"I bought everything I needed, but forgot the eggs!" The old man laughed forcefully. This time there was no pride in his smile, but an inkling of shame and hesitation that he wished to hide. He looked down at the tray.

"I want to see your paintings, sir," Saurabh said, seeing the old man was ashamed of holding the tray.

"Of course," the old man replied. "But, I think now I need to paint something new. The young won't like the old stuff."

"Wonderful idea! It would be a good start. What do you want to paint?"

"Maybe these pigeons when they come back."

"That's a great idea."

"Thank you for the eggs, my son." The old man waddled inside slowly, looking down at the tray of eggs, to put them somewhere safely. He left the window open, maybe it was unintentional. Saurabh knew the old man was not being honest from the very beginning. The van didn't come to their street yesterday. But now the old man was happy to have some eggs.

"Sir!" Saurabh called out loudly. "Look! One pigeon is coming back."

Out of the Ring

Jack unlatched the door of his rented house and, as he opened it, the bell hanging over his head clanged. He never liked it. Cheryl came out of the kitchen. Though he walked in with his shoulders bent and eyes glued to the floor, he saw her coming toward the door.

Outside, it was almost dark, but the wooden floor inside was shining from the evening mopping as dim light reflected through the house. It also offered a pleasant warmth from the cool air outside. The TV was going on in his bedroom, playing old, melodious songs from the '80s. The lyrics of the song fell on his ears as an echo of his past. There was a time when Jack too liked listening to them, while driving or strolling. He recalled those youthful, carefree days of his life in mere seconds.

Cheryl was closer when he looked up. His face was all cut up by the recent fights he had been through. Some blood was still left from today's fight. The left side of his jaw was swollen, and from his left cheekbone to the edge of his eye, a bandage had covered the bruised, purple skin. He handed over his gym bag which contained his uniform, a pair of battered boxing gloves, and a water bottle. When he bent low to untie his ankle-high shoes, he sensed his wife's eyes staring at his trembling hands. Standing upright, he put his hands into the pockets of his jacket. He couldn't decide to take it off or not, but finally did.

"How was it?" Cheryl asked him, while worriedly searching his face.

"What?"

"The fight, of course."

"Oh, the fight!" Putting slippers on his feet and still looking down, Jack said, "Wasn't bad."

Jack embraced his wife like a mundane everyday ritual. He always considered himself too tall to give her a perfect hug. Cheryl kissed him on his chest and held her hands around his hips for a while. After they parted, she took his hands in hers for a closer examination. They were double the size of hers.

"God. It must have been a rough fight," she remarked with compassion. "Are there more injuries, darling?"

"Not much," Jack replied, looking away.

Hands tucked in his pockets, he walked into the drawing room heavy-footed and his wife followed. The gym bag hung from her shoulder and moved back and forth with the movement of her body. She walked smoothly to the slow rhythm of the music playing in the background and put the bag on the table. Before he sat down on the couch, Jack stretched his back left to right as if he were stepping into the ring. Now, his eyes were closed, and his head rested back on the couch. Cheryl stood in front of him, observing him.

"Jack?" She asked. "How was the fight, really?" She sat down close beside him.

"He wasn't quick."

"Thank God! I prayed for that, you know. Did you win, Jack?"

"Of course. I did."

"Oh, my sweetness!" She rubbed her delicate palm on his tough shoulder. "I already knew it. I prayed all day. I hope you too are praying before the game."

"Then, pray to God that they also pay me for each game I win."

"Don't think about the money. You are going to win this tournament and get it."

Jack said nothing and kept his eyes closed and face up toward the ceiling. He spread out his legs a little wider; his body seemed in pursuit of comfort, though his left foot kept tapping on the floor. He was pretending to be sleepy but one could see his restless eyes moving under his darkened eyelids.

"Should I make coffee for you?" Cheryl asked, still rubbing his shoulder.

"No."

"Really, Jack?"

"Sure."

"It's your usual time for a cup of coffee, isn't it? And as you often mention, it's good for your muscle ache."

"Now, I'm fine."

"But, you said, things must happen at the right time..."

"Please, Cheryl." Jack pulled her hand off his shoulder and put it on the couch beside his head. "I don't really feel like having coffee right now. And, please turn that TV off. I hate these bloody, old songs."

Cheryl waited a moment, then went in the other room to turn off the TV. It was quiet for a moment, then Jack heard the gentle tinkling of the wind chimes above their porch and the faint rustle of the trees just beyond their house. Cheryl shuffled to the kitchen to check on something and came back after a little while. Cleaning her hands on her apron, she stood there. She found her tired husband sitting in the same slack position in which she'd left him.

"Jack?" she asked.

"What?"

"Aren't you forgetting something?" She was curious and perplexed at the same time.

"I'll change later. I'm fine. No need to put ointment on." He talked to her with his eyes closed.

"If you're hungry, we can have dinner. It's ready. Today, we have a cake too. I made it myself. Why? Think for yourself and don't ask me what day it is today," she said, laughing intentionally.

As Jack opened his eyes, Cheryl moved her gaze away from his aching face to the clay pot hanging outside of the window. In that pot used to be a little Basil plant, but it had withered away during the last winter. Her eyes came back to her husband with a forced smile on her face, as if she wanted to say something, but Jack didn't ask her anything. Instead, he looked down at his toes. He had started to say that he was done with having dinner in the same way every night. In the fear of making her more uncomfortable, he changed his mind before speaking.

"Yes, dinner!" he said. "Let's have dinner." He stood up, trudged to the dining room, and sat down on the edge of his chair. Elbows on the table, he began tapping his left foot again. He looked at the pattern of the tablecloth in the same way a sailor caught in the middle of a storm would look at the map ruined by the seawater and the weather.

Cheryl prepared the table, not turning the overhead lights on. Instead, she lit three candles, and while serving him, tried to glance into his eyes as if wanting to hear something kind tonight. She had beautiful brown eyes—appealing. Wearing eyeshadows and eyeliners all day hid the fat around her eyes and made them look calm and ageless. Jack always adored them but today they were frightening.

She sat down near him. They started eating. She loved to eat while the food was hot, but Jack started late. While eating the roasted chicken, garnished with cooked peas, mashed potatoes, and caramelized onions—which was the French way of having a chicken—she talked about many things he knew nothing about.

"You aren't listening to me," she ended. "Okay! Let's eat first, then talk."

Strangely, it was confusing for Jack to distinguish between a fork and a knife, as though he was a boy of no more than five and needed some lessons on table manners. At last, he picked up the spoon. He took a mouthful of soup.

"It's still hot." Jack let the spoon rest beside the soup bowl and glared down at the edge of the knife while he tried to twist it on the table. Finding Cheryl looking at him, he put the knife down and started on the chicken. They had been eating canned food for almost two weeks, but the greasy taste of a homemade chicken, which he liked, made no visible difference on his face. He said not a word about the chicken. Soon there was a film on the top of the soup and, before it started to congeal completely, he began to guzzle it down in haste. He finished, leaving a trail of red beads on the tablecloth between him and his bowl. Cheryl regarded his trembling hand while he took hold of the glass of water. He put the glass down and found his wife's eyes still studying him; their intensity was scaring him to death.

"What's the matter, Jack?" she finally asked.

"Sorry for messing it all up."

"Forget about the mess," she answered. "We always talk when we eat. We talk about things that matter and that don't matter, but we always talk. You tell me the weird stories from the gym and I tell what the ladies in our neighborhood were gossiping about. Mostly we talk about the food. You don't think twice before you criticize if it's bad and appreciate it if it's good. Moreover, you've always asked me to cook chicken in a French way. It's your favorite dish. But today, something is bothering you—what's wrong, Jack? Tell me please."

While she was speaking to him, Jack maintained a tough, blank, defensive look on his face, which made her look down in desperation. She stirred the spoon in her half-filled bowl of soup.

"I'm scared, Jack. You know how much I love you."

"I know it all right. You shouldn't be concerned otherwise."

"I can't help it."

"Darling! I am just not feeling well today. Maybe it's the air outside."

"You said you are fine."

"I am fine, but... " Jack shook his head and dropped it down into his cupped palms. "I'm so sorry." He stood up. "I'm going out for a walk. I don't want to ruin your evening."

"It's *our* evening, Jack," she said. "I thought we could have a little drink today. And there's a cake too. How can I forget it? You know what day is today?"

For the first time, Jack noticed a foil-wrapped bottle placed on the table and two glasses shining in the candlelight.

"Jack, it's been too long since we've had a drink together. But today is different. Can we please...?" The words came out of her mouth with a hint of hesitation and her lips quivered.

"You are so kind, but I don't think I need any wine just now," said Jack. "A little walk will be enough. For sure."

Jack left the table. Putting on his jacket and his shoes, he came over and kissed her on the back of her head. He didn't look at her face.

"Take care of yourself, darling," Cheryl said, looking at his retreating figure.

* * *

As Jack stepped out of the apartment, he despised the bell over his head that never stopped clanging. It reminded him of something unpleasant. Like every other antique piece that stuffed the walls and the corners of every room in his house. They were all his wife's choice. Cheryl loved ancient-looking things and they bought many fine copies of originals. Jack had considered them boring, though he always found himself getting bored around new things too. Old or new, he was bored all the time. He strode through the street and there, after the first left, he stopped. He took out a cigarette. *Sorry, Cheryl,* he said to himself, and lit it, then walked leisurely on, puffing on it. He inhaled the smoke as if, after this, he was going to quit smoking forever. There was a cloud of smoke hanging over his shoulder visible under the streetlights. Every car that drove by had to honk twice or thrice and then someone, leaning out of the window, would swear at him. Jack kept strolling carelessly through the stinking urine-soaked streets of the city until he reached Michael's.

Inside, he sat at the only empty table by a window, thinking about an old man he had just found sitting on the bench right outside the bar. *I've seen him somewhere before.* He put his head down on his folded arms on the table and didn't even care to raise it even when the waitress came to take his order. He glanced around a few minutes later when she came back and poured him a glass of beer, smiling at him. She recognized him. A few days ago hundreds of flyers with his and his opponent's photographs had been distributed in the area. And, there was also a billboard about the fight at the main road, outside the street. Everybody in the neighborhood knew who Jack was.

At the far end of the bar sat Raghu with three of his buddies, all cheering and laughing. Jack could see Raghu's busted, red face from where he sat. Jack had knocked him out earlier today in the ring, but he didn't look defeated anymore. They noticed Jack.

"Look! The winner has joined the losers," declared Raghu, raising the glass in the air towards Jack. "Let's celebrate in the name of our next world champion, and me, the champion of all losers," he said sarcastically. People laughed. Unconcerned, Jack continued drinking.

Raghu, a short, bulky man, more of a local bully than a boxer, stood up and swaggered toward Jack. His three friends followed, rolling up their sleeves, preparing themselves for something terrible. Raghu sat his fat ass on a chair near Jack and looked at him.

"You must be celebrating here," Raghu said, staring into Jack's eyes.

"None of your business, Raghu," Jack replied.

"We only want to pay tribute to the victor."

"Go away. Please!"

"Please!?" Raghu laughed. "What a victorious way to respond to your opponent." Raghu turned his bald head toward his ugly friends.

"Not here, Raghu."

"Here or there, it doesn't matter," Raghu sneered. "You think you're better because you beat me in the ring?" Putting both his hands on the table, Raghu glared deep into Jack's eyes. "Show me here and now if you are."

The waitress watched them from a good distance with a tray in her hands. Two other waiters peeked from over her shoulder, anticipating something expensive. All the patrons in the bar exchanged glances, but Jack kept his eyes locked with Raghu's. He stood up. Raghu stood too, rolling up the sleeves of his dull, wine-stinking, checkered shirt. Jack looked past him and then at the waitress. She was startled. A drop of sweat rolled down the back of Jack's neck. He looked around, then all at once, stepped back.

"I'm not in the mind for any row here," he said. "Meet me tomorrow in the ring, if you want to test me again." He took his bottle off the table and went to the bar to pay the bill. He didn't look at Raghu while he walked out.

Jack heard them all laughing inside and calling him names. He was no longer a winner for them. But the tall, old man sitting on the outside bench simpered at him. That hurt Jack the most.

When you want the victory, you think the victory will make you happy. But this isn't the case. You are gloomy when you have nothing and you remain the same even after getting what you want. The bloody nature of human beings. You fall or rise. Does it matter if we are condemned to be like this?

Church bells rang while Jack lumbered through the street, talking to himself, swinging the bottle in his hand, stopping and taking a drink every few steps. Soon the bottle was emptied and he smashed it on the iron pole displaying a U-turn sign.

"Fuck this city!" Jack cursed as he entered his house. "And this damn bell too."

The TV was on. Cheryl was watching a decent family show that would raise a little laughter every once in a while, that is if you are not too stressed and are eager to laugh. As soon as Jack came into the room, Cheryl turned the TV off. She looked carefully at him from head to toe. He walked around the bed and sat down, light-headed and still sweating.

"Are you drunk?" she asked.

"No." Jack lay down.

"Did you fight with someone outside?"

"NO. I am not supposed to fight out of the ring."

"Jack, listen! I want to ask you something."

"Yes, please."

"Are you worried about something? I mean the rent, bills, fees or something like that? Are you worried about money?"

Jack said nothing.

"Dear, listen!" She continued. "Everything's gonna be all right. Don't worry about money or anything else. God has His grand plan and we will all be saved. We're still young with sufficient time to make things right."

"Sure!"

"You are not listening, darling."

"I was thinking about something else."

"Then tell me about it."

"I don't want to burden you, Cheryl."

"Tell me, if you truly love me." She grabbed his hand.

"Okay then," Jack said.

Cheryl dragged herself closer, put her hand on his thigh, then rubbed it gently.

"Do you know Kapil?" Jack began, "The young boy I've been training?"

"I don't think I..."

"Anyway, he killed himself last night."

"What?"

"Yeah! They said last night he slit open his wrist with a blade, and one side of his body was soaked in his own blood when they found him."

"Jesus Christ!" She couldn't speak for a while, then she checked her husband's eyes. "How old was he?"

"At least ten years younger than me. I used to teach him in my leisure time. He was just a good lad."

"Why did he do such a thing? He must have a father, or a mother, or a sister, or at least someone who loved him. It's a crime. A sin. He broke the law of God. No one in his kingdom should commit such a hateful crime. It's unforgivable! Didn't he know? How can one even think about killing oneself?"

"It's not that easy, Cheryl."

"It is! Life is an easy thing. God made it easy for us."

Jack sighed in disappointment. They didn't speak for a couple of minutes and their heads hung low. Meanwhile, it was the silence that came in through the curtains and crawled onto the bed and climbed up their shoulders, and spoke to them in their ears in a very cruel manner. Cheryl took a deep breath and let it go.

"Anyway!" she said, staring down at Jack's hand, now placed on the bed, "We should pray for him." Then, she closed her eyes and opened them after a minute. "It wasn't your fault, Jack."

"I envied him all the time."

"Why?"

"He was quicker and more ambitious. I thought he'd join the league faster than his peers."

"We don't really know what God has decided for us. No one knows! God works in mysterious ways. You must stop thinking about it. It wasn't your fault."

"I envied him, that's troubling me."

"Have faith in God. Ask for his forgiveness if that's bothering you. He must have been a good kid."

"I was jealous of him," Jack repeated, but this time the words hardly came out of his mouth as though his throat was caught up by something.

"Oh, my good husband. My lovely dearest one. You have a heart of gold. I'm glad you're my husband. But please do not think about that, please."

"We must sleep now, it's late," Jack said after a pause. It wasn't a good suggestion.

"Did you take a pill? You also forgot it yesterday," Cheryl asked.

"I don't feel like taking anything. I'm fine."

"Jack, are you sure?" she asked as she slid down slowly in between his arms.

"Yes, Cheryl."

"Can I do anything that may soothe you?" She squeezed his shirt in her hand while her other hand rubbed his back.

"No, Cheryl, not today."

* * *

His wife fell asleep in a matter of a few minutes, whereas Jack couldn't, for hours. He stared at the hands of the clock hanging in front of him and began counting the seconds in his mind in order to forget about everything else. It wasn't working. The opposite was happening. Every four or five minutes he would forget where he was and had to start over. He thought about the time he had spent in the ring; the time when he was young and trained laboriously; and the month in which he quarreled every day with his wife. Then, about the days when Cheryl went through the first few weeks of pregnancy. All the while he was counting. Jack once had been exactly like Kapil. *No, Kapil was quicker than me.* Jack was agile enough and fearless in the ring but now he was afraid of forgetting the count. His chest swelled up. As a young, sweating yellow face with smiling lips floated ahead of his eyes in the dark, no longer could he see the clock and he lost the count again. He sat up in bed.

Turning on the lamp, he saw Cheryl's face. She was sleeping under his stretched-out shadow. Her mouth was open, her neat hands placed on her stomach. He looked down at his own hands which were rough, full of cuts and bruises. Placing his hands on his chest, he felt his heart beating through his shirt. *I shouldn't do it.* Before getting up, he took heavy deep breaths twice, as if bracing himself up for a fight. He went to the kitchen and got some water, which felt so cold moving down his throat that he thought his lungs would freeze. He noticed his hand shaking while drinking.

In the hallway, he saw his reflection in the window glass. The harsh, night wind was banging the bell outside and the branches of the trees were snapping, and the twinkling of wind chimes... all together created a music, an unpleasant music. Jack went closer to the window. The weather had drastically changed. He noticed a shadow outside. Apparently, a tall man with a lean, strong physique was strolling in front of his house despite the bad weather. Jack couldn't see his face precisely, but he knew by heart that he was the same old man he had seen outside the bar. The shadow stopped moving and looked toward him. Jack drew the curtains shut.

He ran to the bathroom, panting as if he had just finished a fight. He washed his face in the sink, looked at himself in the mirror, and then closed his eyes and looked again—a fleshless bony structure full of scars. There, as he recalled Kapil again, he saw the glimpse of his own shaking hand. He thought of the pills! In the chest, there was a small white container. "A Pill Every Night Before Sleeping," it said. Jack opened the cap and took out six of them. They looked bright red against the pinkish-white of his palm, then he clenched them hard in his fist. *How strange! The things that calm your mind can also kill you.* He heard his wife snoring in the bedroom when he studied his face again. He hated it. All of it. All the scars. All of his life. He couldn't figure out what piece of this puzzle called life was truly missing. Having searched for years, looking from every angle, he was convinced that he would never find it. *That makes Kapil right.* With pills inside his fist, he looked again into the mirror. It wasn't himself who looked back; it was that scary, old man. He punched on the wall next to the mirror, then he put all the pills back into the container, except for one. It was hard to keep just one.

He swallowed it down with water. Coming out into the living room, he looked behind the door and saw the calendar that the gym gave every member as a gift each new year. He ran his fingertip through the past dates of the month thinking how fast time can pass. Then, his finger stopped. Today was the last day of this tedious month. *The last day of November!* He repeated it to himself. He was taken aback by a sudden realization.

Jack went back to the bedroom. Nervous, he stopped in the doorway.

"Cheryl!?" He was startled to see his wife was sitting up in bed.

"Where have you been?" Her eyes were fully awake as if she had been scared by the thunder or a nightmare.

"Just went to drink some water, nothing else."

"Are you trying to do that again?"

"No way."

"Show me your pockets."

"I'm not hiding any pills in them, believe me. I won't ever." He stepped forward and turned his pockets inside out to prove himself.

"Oh, Jack... I trust you," she said in a low tone. "You won't believe what I just saw. It was the worst nightmare of my life."

"What was it?"

"It's gone now, Jack." Cheryl pulled Jack closer and took his body into her arms, her lips pressing on his stomach. "Just stay close to me."

"How could I forget our anniversary?" he asked sorrowfully. "I'm sorry."

They felt at ease with each other again.

"Oh, Jack! Let's not talk about it, it's past."

They lay down in each other's arms.

"Yes, it's past," said Jack.

A City on Fire

The city was said to be the most glorious city in the world and in the history of the world, proudly made of pure gold. But that night a giant shadow flew above its gold-plated domes and towers with high-hanging gargoyles. Later, all that was remarkable about the city was that it had been completely destroyed and it sunk into an ever-expanding fire.

In its last days, flames had moved, like red demons with thousands of yellow hands, across the city. They swallowed everything that came in their way. Eventually, there was nothing beautiful about the city except the stars above. Sadly, no one cared to look at the stars; people were running across the streets, regretting their past crimes, screaming as their clothes caught fire. Many died while asleep in their beds as half-burned timbers from the roofs fell onto them mercilessly. They blamed it all on the sins of their king as they screamed for the very last time. In moments, the cries filled the streets of the city. A cloud of smoke enshrouded it, hiding the stars, leaving no beauty.

In spite of all this, many lonely souls had come and sat in the inn on the western outskirts of the city at their regular time on their regular benches to savor their regular drink. But, strangely today, no one talked about politics, drought, or wars and no one clinked the mugs with each other. They sat there without even moving their heads, trying to refrain themselves from looking out of the only window in the inn. It made them look like cold-blooded non-humans. Out there, the fear might have driven them crazy. But inside the walls of the inn, they felt safe, busy with the trivial act of sipping the *Soma,* and it kept them within the boundaries of their sanity.

Diyon, a fifteen-year-old soldier, also sat there among them in the company of one of his senior officers, Purushottam. Purushottam had been the former commander of the infantry unit that was trained to kill enemies with spears. He was great with the spear but due to his irregular drinking, he was politely dismissed from his position. Afterward, he liked to train the young soldiers and was seen as one of the most respected men in the whole army. He had always been an easygoing person. But today, he also looked out of his mind as he kept pouring *Soma* into his copper mug instead of joining the rest of the soldiers trying to save the city.

Further off, in the southern part of the city, tall statues of royal ancestors were burning like gigantic torches in hell. Their gold was melting down and the sharply carved features of their faces disappeared, making them look like distorted, weeping demons.

Diyon was the only one looking out the window. It hurt his eyes, yet he kept looking at the fire.

Is this the end? He lowered his eyes and shook his head, holding it in his palms, lamenting.

"They hate us!" Diyon muttered, still looking down.

"Everybody hates his enemy," said Purushottam, who was sitting in front of him with his bruised elbows on the table. "Nothing new about it."

"This is a different kind of hating, sir."

"Oh, what's the difference?"

"I don't know," said Diyon, still looking down. He looked up into the drunken eyes of his senior. "I don't like the fact that they call us demons. We can be anything but demons."

"Why do you think they call us demons?"

"Maybe because we don't worship their gods," Diyon said, looking down at the two spears that leaned against his chair, pointing at him. Terrified, he moved his finger on the wetness of his mug while holding onto it. But he didn't like the idea of drinking *Soma* when the whole of his city was being consumed by flames.

"Don't you know," Purushottam said as he refilled his mug from the pitcher. "We worship the same black lingam god, whom the prince had worshipped at the shore with his young arrogant brother. That was before they asked the god of the ocean to give them a way to cross it. Didn't you hear this story? Have you ever thought: how would they cross the vast ocean without any ships? We are unaware of their powers and this fire is just an example for us. Mark my words! They're going to cross the ocean sometime soon and come to us to slit our sinful throats." He ended with a laughter that echoed in the inn. Everyone around looked at his scared face for a moment, then they were again drowned in their mugs. "Better we have as many drinks as possible before we die either by the fire or by the war. Death is now inevitable."

Diyon said nothing and turned his head towards the window again to have another pitiful glance at the chaos. It was now too hot to look at. The old man who owned this place, a master of making the best *Soma* in the city, came in with a big copper pitcher in his shaking hand. Today, he was letting them drink anything, cheap or expensive, without a penny. He placed the pitcher on the table and Purushottam lifted it to refill his mug.

"It's delicious," he said as he sipped the sweetness of the preserved plant juice from the mug, closing his eyes. "Thank you for one more free drink," he told the old man. The old man went away without answering. He seemed deaf tonight. But Diyon could recall him answering all of his clients, asking for more money in the least polite way just a few days ago. He knew things had changed in a matter of a day.

"I said, have as many drinks as you can before dying," repeated the dismissed officer. "We all are going to die anyway."

"The fire was unpredictable, sir," Diyon said with rare confidence. "But they don't stand a chance against us on the battlefield even though they could somehow cross the ocean, which is next to impossible."

"What makes you think that, child?" Purushottam laughed at him, almost throwing his wine out. He put down his mug with a thud.

"Our king!" said Diyon, proudly. "I have never heard of such a great king in my life. Not in the history of our island nor beyond, even in the history of *Bharatvarsh* after the great king Rishabha who turned into a saint a thousand years ago."

"Our king *was* indeed the most powerful king," Purushottam said. "And, there *was* a time when every other king across the world was afraid of him. So afraid that there are still stories about him having ten heads, ha-ha. A king with ten heads! Can you imagine how scared our neighbors were?" He guffawed and took another long drink from his mug. After he put it down on the table, he remained silent for a moment.

"Maybe he was the greatest king after Rishabha," Purushottam continued solemnly as his eyes narrowed. "But only until now, when the desire to get a woman ruined him."

"But aren't we all ruined by something?" Diyon asked in reply. "That doesn't make us demons."

"Yes, but he is being ruined by a woman. That is different. The lust for that foreign woman has ruined our king. Nobody would say it because we are all afraid of his and his brothers' powers, but I would say it loudly to everyone. I am not afraid of anything and ready to die. Here, I tell you: Everyone, we have already lost our king, lost this war." He put his arm wide across the chair, wiping his wet mustache with the back of his other hand, and laughed ruefully.

"Maybe...or maybe not," Diyon said, considering the drunken commoners. Their faces floated in the light that occasionally came in from outside, light that was sometimes as dim as candlelight and sometimes like a sudden, ghastly flash. Sitting motionless, none of them looked like humans anymore, he thought.

"You know what ruined me?" Purushottam asked abruptly.

"What, sir?"

"Fighting! Fought more than twenty battles in my life. Won most of them. But it ruined me. Defeat doesn't ruin you. It only makes you prepare for something better. But, victory! Victory, when it gets to your head, ruins everything." He paused thoughtfully. "You're too young to understand it."

"I am."

"But, one day you will understand everything in case you remain alive after this war." He took his mug and drank the rest in a single draught.

"Maybe I'll stay alive," answered Diyon. He watched the older soldier guzzling down the wine again. Then he studied the stiff faces of the other men sitting with mugs in their hands. He noticed that the commoners suddenly stopped drinking as a great flash came from outside that was bright enough to blind all of them for a moment. He couldn't look at them anymore.

"We must go out and join others now," Diyon suggested.

"Listen! War is the worst thing we do. I tell you. Why did Rishabha become a saint? You better not throw yourself into this fight now," said Purushottam. "We've already lost it, you see outside?"

"We are soldiers. It's our duty," Diyon told him.

"Staying alive is the only duty we have as humans," the senior said dismissively and drank another mug. "I am going to leave this city if this fire fails to kill me tonight."

"Isn't that cowardly?!"

"Boy! Haven't you witnessed what a single shadow did to this once unassailable city? The over-passionate love for a foreign woman has ruined our king, our city, the entire kingdom. All you need to do is to drink and stay away from women and this war. That won't make you a stupid ten-headed demon like our king." Purushottam laughed.

Diyon considered him with disgust.

"Sir, then *I* must go," Diyon said.

"What ruined you, Deevam?" asked the officer without listening to him.

"I am Diyon," he said. "You have drunk enough. sir. Let's go do our duty."

"Tell me, what ruined you?"

"I don't know," Diyon replied. "See, for now, I am done." He stood up.

"Drink more! You may not drink anything after tonight."

"My gut is already burning."

"You must learn to stand things."

"But I cannot sit here anymore. I must go."

While the officer lifted another mug to drink, Diyon lifted his spear and went out without looking back at his drunken and ruined officer.

As he stepped out of the inn's main door, he found the flames as high as the tallest war elephant, inching towards him. All the gold of the city had been licked by this burning demon. Whichever corner his sight fell upon, only deathly cries were coming to him, deafening his ears. He didn't know which direction he should go first. Once, he thought of going back into the inn and emptying some more mugs of wine with Purushottam. He must have a plan to flee from the city without being burnt in the fire. That was the safest and cleverest choice. The city was already ruined, maybe by the desire of getting a woman or by the arrogance of his so-called ten-headed king or by a mysterious shadow or by misfortune. He couldn't undo it.

He stood there with his eyes closed for a few seconds, feeling the heat directly on his face. His flesh began to redden. There were more flames when he opened his eyes again. He stepped ahead, towards the fire and the cries, to save whatever he once admired about the city. He just wanted to prove to himself that he wasn't a demon!

Separation Anxiety

All the while, I was aware of what would happen with Jakie later. Being just a dog, he could not understand. He had been trailing Seema all around the house since she had worn that perfume. His insecurity returned and grasped him wholly as he followed us into the bedroom and saw the bags were packed. He investigated the room sniffing, inspecting corner to corner, as if it was a new territory to explore, and climbed up on the bed.

"You are going crazy," I told him. He jumped off the bed and sat down at Seema's feet.

Seema, wearing her newly purchased overcoat, had been sitting next to me on the edge of the bed for fifteen minutes without uttering a word. Her hand was in mine; our hands were resting in my lap. Her handbag and luggage were placed beside her left foot, propped against the bed, waiting to be picked up and carried out.

Two weeks ago, Seema had first indicated her desire to go back to Bangalore to spend time with her sisters and friends in a warmer place; it had started getting cold up here in Uttrakhand. With a different pretext each time, I objected. However, after supper last night, while discussing what should be done with Jakie if we go out again to earn a living, she began to pack.

Our light-hearted argument had turned into a typical marital feud, all too frequent during the lockdown. It was followed by a long, cold, sleepless night. Early this morning she took a hot shower, then sat at the dresser before I had even rolled out of bed. She had obviously made a decision. We had morning coffee together, looking out the window at the fog.

"It's getting late!" Seema said and stood up. Jakie imitated her, clutched her overcoat's sleeve in his mouth, and pulled her back. She frowned and said, "He should understand."

"He wants you to stay a little longer," I said. Looking at Jakie, Seema sat down again in frustration. Jakie, too, sat down on the floor, close to the luggage as if guarding it. While his head lay down on his left leg, his erect ears frequently changed directions to every little noise, his copper-brown eyes scrutinizing each sound that echoed from the walls.

"He's a poor little dog," I said, looking down at Jakie.

"We've got our lives too, don't we? And we are meant to live them," said Seema. "And now, since we can go out finally, we must live it."

"He doesn't like to be without us. Isn't it sweet?"

"Well, it's rather irritating."

"But..."

"But what? He's seven, don't you know?" she blurted out. "It's been seven years. It seems sometimes he is an unnecessary burden to us, to our lives! Pardon me for saying that, but it's true—we are caged in this house all the time with him, can't you see?" Seema stopped, shaking her head ruefully. Lifting her hands in an agitated gesture, she looked around as though she was cursing the walls. "We never took a moment to teach him that he's got a life without us too. But yes, it is my fault as much as it is yours."

I remained silent, partly because that was the way I always acted in her presence, and partly because she was right. We never trained him when we had the time to do so. It was all fun, all the time, we were busy playing with him and carrying him wherever we went. He was just a mere puppy. But now what a pity!

"Even if we leave fifteen minutes later," I said as I grabbed Seema's hand, "I'll make sure we get there on time." I put my arm around her, feeling the tender skin on the back of her neck.

"We must leave now," she said, removing my hand and looking up at the clock on the wall, which seemed to pace faster than it should.

But I took her in my arms and let my head rest on her shoulder for a while. Her perfume was enthralling, like some old Malbec wine. Had she not worn the overcoat over the shirt, I'd have started undressing her right away. The overcoat and the shirt inside were not a big deal though (it was way easier than removing the skin-tight jeans in a public bathroom in the middle of a cold night). But after looking at the clock ticking unfavorably, I changed my mind. Her reddened lips parted to say something, but before she could say it, I laid my lips on hers.

It wasn't a long kiss. But I couldn't remember the last time we locked our lips like this. Later, I sucked my lips in desperation. Her hands slipped away from mine. The moment she pulled herself back, Jakie began to whimper. It was a low squeaking sound, capable of sending depressing chills that froze me on the spot. No wonder I spent days and nights lying beside him in the bed, or even on the floor sometimes after COVID-19 had broken out and snatched my job away during the total lockdown, when we had been isolated in our home. The lockdown had ended just a few days ago. Now it was over, and life could start all over again—if you believe it. Strangely, I couldn't yet believe it was over.

"I'm sorry," Seema said, peeking into Jakie's rheumy eyes. "Poor dog," she patted his head, then got up and walked to the door. Jakie stood up too. After staring at her face, looking for a sign, his ears now dropped low in submission. His tongue stuck out, lolling, and a few beads of saliva, falling from his mouth, made a row on the brown carpeted floor as he went closer to rub his head against her knee. One could see how anxious he had become just by looking at the handbag hanging from her shoulder.

I've learned from experience it was better to avoid Jakie's silent pleadings while leaving him behind than to pat him and whisper good words. We went out; he followed us to the door anyway. After succeeding in pushing his head inside with my knee, I slammed the door shut and locked it. Through the glass, that also reflected my worn-out face and scattered graying hairs of my early thirties, the poor dog saw me. I went out carrying the bag, determined.

Once in the car, I turned to face our house. It was painted white and sea-green. When we had planned the house nine years ago, Seema fancied making the windows on the ground floor higher, but I objected, changed the design myself, and kept the windows low. Through one of them, I could make out a dark brown figure now tilting his head as the half-dried leaves of the myrtle tree in our small garden were blocking his view. He started scratching the panel where it was already ruined by his claws.

I lowered my eyes, rubbing lightly on the leather of the steering wheel with my thumb.

"The more you wait, the more he cries," warned Seema.

"All right," I agreed, though my ears imagined a hint of a canine shriek dwelling in the thin morning air.

We drove off through streets submerged in the crispy grayness of a late November morning.

I changed the direction of the mirror, remembering how Seema had kept the same hairstyle for all these years. But now it was tied behind in a low bun, making her look a bit different. Even so, an urge to touch her, to feel her exposed neck, struck my mind. While shifting gears, I intentionally brushed Seema's hand with mine, and finally, she regarded me with a smile. I slid my hand into her lap and steered with the other. I held her hand. Slowly our hands became warm. I wanted to say something to her, my chest was swelling up with the prolonged thought. She continued scrolling down the over-brightened screen of her mobile phone, not smiling anymore. Right then, I imagined I heard the high-pitched howl of Jakie's separation, though I knew we were too far away to actually hear it. Still, it was heart-wrenching.

This morning the road was quite busy. I've always been cautious, even when it was empty, but today I couldn't keep my eyes forward. I kept looking out the window for a glimpse of stray dogs. Unfortunately, there were many. In this part of the city where we lived, there was a hell of a lot of stray dogs. From our house, whichever direction you turn, you would spot them in packs, growling and eating the wasted food humans left for them.

As I turned left onto the main road, I noticed a starving lapdog sitting by the footpath. My eyes were captivated by the way he was licking the maggot wounds on his hairy back. All of a sudden, as soon as I looked back to the road, I jerked Seema's hand away to hold the steering wheel steady with both of my hands and put on the brakes. The wheels screeched, and the car stopped.

Ahead of me, about a meter away, was a black puppy, walking briskly on his tiny paws towards his mother, who was anxiously waiting for him at the footpath. It was a wide lane. Many small and large vehicles were crossing it. But nobody cared to slow down to give the little puppy the necessary space and safety for it to cross. No one really cared if their actions made someone, even a dog, feel insecure about their life. On the contrary, some took pleasure in it.

The pup looked malnourished and reminded me of the day we took Jakie home seven years ago. The careless driver of a scooter had run over him, giving him bruises, fractures, and cuts all over his body. He was unable to stand upright, and lay there alone to die on the road. When we found him, he was fighting for his life, breathing rapidly as if someone was pumping the air into his baby lungs—or, more precisely, taking it away. I lifted his bloodied body with my bare hands and took him to a veterinary clinic nearby. There, he was put under medical observation for 72 hours. Later, at home, we fed him with the nutritious diet a puppy needed. When he was able to walk again, we inquired about him around the same place where we found him injured. We learned that his mother had died in a fatal car accident, and all of her pups died of ailments or starvation in the winter nights except the one we had in our hands. We decided to adopt him, as we always wanted a pet, and raise him like our own child.

Looking at this frightened puppy now, terrified by the ruthless traffic, yet trying to reach his mother, I had an impulse to get out and carry him to his mother, to ultimate safety. I turned to look at my wife. Her face showed an unusual indifference. The way she had been complaining about the time left me with nothing to say or do but to resume driving and leave the puppy on his own poor luck.

We arrived at the station, and I parked the car thinking of Jakie and the puppy, so it took more time than necessary. The tightened muscles around Seema's eyes proved it. I was panting as if I had been running, though I had just gotten out of the car. As we walked into the station, my heart kept racing.

The railway station looked outlandishly gray, and way less noisy than the last time I was here. We were scanned at the entrance. Walking to our platform, I heard a lady announcing arrivals and departures of the trains, along with how the rules of traveling had changed since the pandemic. Her voice, though young and gentle, caused my blood to surge with anticipation each time she mentioned the name of a city or a station. But, five minutes into our plodding toward the platform, passing a few travelers who were eager to move out of the way when they noticed our masked faces, I didn't really hear the young lady say anything about *Bangalore*. That made me smile inwardly. Many trains were canceled without prior notification. I thought how joyful Jakie would be if Seema returned home with me.

But the departures projected on the screens over our heads erased my smile. The train to Bangalore was shown to be delayed, not canceled. Seema and I looked at it angrily. We inquired about the train at the ticket window and the double-chinned man inside first yawned and then laughed, explaining satirically why they hung up those wide screens and how much stress he would have if people stopped having good eyes. We moved on.

"Let's go and wait there," I suggested, signifying the wide-open glass door of the not-so-clean-looking waiting room. Seema's face showed her unwillingness, but there was no other choice.

The waiting room was warm and cozy, with twenty rows of steel benches; their metallic edges reflected the light of the thin sunlight that came in through the huge windows.

Seema simply sat down on a bench a little away from me, talking to someone on her phone, swearing about the delayed trains with jerks of her hand. Cold hesitant flames rose from my gut when I thought of sitting by her. She was still my wife after all. Anyway, I sat there, and she eventually ended the call.

"She's also mad at the trains," Seema said to me.

"Yes, she must be," I nodded.

Shifting toward her, I put my arm around her and asked her to put her head on my shoulder if she could. She did. This pleasant warmth of closeness between us had always been soothing for me, but this time I just shivered.

"Should we have coffee?" I asked her. "I feel cold."

To the right of us was a canteen. I waved, and a waiter came over. A strange, multi-colored muffler was tightly wrapped around his gaunt neck. Looking at it caused a painful fluttering in my stomach. He seemed in a hurry when he came to take our order.

"My boss gave me this beautiful muffler," he said. breathing rapidly. Then he stopped to breathe again before he went away. I wished he'd take a long time to deliver our order so I could be with Seema for a little more.

Outside, a blue train came on the first track but passed the station swiftly with an aerodynamic sound that lasted a few seconds. The next train on the other track came slower and stopped with an irritating screech of the wheels which somehow matched that of my whimpering dog. Passengers rushed to board it. I felt uneasy and turned to look at Seema.

In that moment against my arm, her body looked stunningly alluring. Her breast was firmly pressed against the thick cloth. I began to rub her shoulder, feeling her creamy skin through the layer of her overcoat. I was dying to tell her something, whisper some words to her, but then the waiter came with our coffees and I couldn't. We picked up the cups. Unlike my wife, I sipped slowly, looking out of the window at the fog and tracks that had emptied again. The cup was warm and pleasant to hold.

"He must be whining madly by now, you know?" I said to Seema, just to break the silence.

"Yes, I know," Seema snapped, pouring out her frustration at the delayed trains and other things on me. "You think I don't?"

"Of course you do! I didn't mean that," I tried to explain.

"You said it as if I don't care."

"You do care, darling. With all my heart I know."

"Don't talk like this, at least not when I'm leaving."

"Okay. But, I didn't mean what you are thinking. I mean – oh, I just don't know what I mean," I stammered. "It's just that you are going, I guess, I am losing my mind." I shook my head.

"It's simple," she replied. "Just don't think so much." Putting down the empty cup on the table, she studied herself in the window glass, rubbing her lips together. As I looked at the pout of her lower lip, I fantasized about kissing her. But the very next thought forced me to reconsider my desires. I saw myself in the glass. I seemed to be sleepy and old, rubbing my eyes with my index finger and thumb.

"It's not easy to stop thinking," I said as though complaining about something I don't know.

"That's the real problem," Seema replied. "It's crippling you. It will be good for Jakie too, if he learns to keep calm when left alone."

"He's too old to learn anything new," I said as the image of his graying muzzle floated in front of me.

"It's too early for a dog to go gray," the thin, calm man told me the last time we took him to the vet for his regular check-up and vaccination. "Aren't you feeding him as suggested? Eggs? Sweet potatoes? A few drops of salmon oil in the food?" The doctor made a perplexed face, rubbed his stubble, and continued, "This dog of yours is suffering, but I don't know why." Only later, when I Googled about dogs going gray at an early age, did I find out what the doctor couldn't tell us, and what Jakie was really suffering from – separation anxiety!

"Now, while I'll be gone, you and the dog will have plenty of time to learn anything, new or old," said Seema, glancing down at her wrist. It was rude. So, like any other time, to not make a dismal situation, I said nothing. I just swallowed my thoughts and closed my eyes to forget them; most of the time it worked.

"We should go outside and walk," Seema said as she stood up. "This waiting is too much. The coffee has made it worse." I stood up and lifted her bag.

Passing through a lighted passage with dirty tiles under our creaking shoes, we took an overpass. The tracks below us went in both directions as far as my eyes could see and all of them were empty, but I could hear a train whistle coming from the west. While descending the steps on the other side, I heard the lady over the speaker mentioning "Bangalore" twice or perhaps thrice. A few people walking wearily next to us broke away from their yawning and made a quick leap toward platform number seven. As the train pulled in, the lady finished saying the train to Bangalore had just arrived and would be departing at 9:40—only five minutes from now.

People almost ran. Seema was jumpy. Unlike her, the news turned my legs into pillars of cold steel. She wanted me to walk as fast as others. But without a thought, I grabbed her arm and drew her back to me.

"He's gonna miss you a lot," I said, staring deep into her widened eyes as if searching for something. The words had just come out of my mouth, but that's all I could manage to say.

"You'll take care of him," she said, raising her brows. "I'll miss him too," she added as I noticed her lips had dried up. I craved to moisten them with mine, but she walked away. I stared at her moving shoulder, the bun, and the overcoat, all disappearing in the wave of the crowd.

With her heavy bag in my hand, I jostled my way through. My eyes tried to catch a glimpse of her. Soon I found myself panting. The noise of hundreds of shoes agitated my ears. No longer did I want to listen to the soft voice of the lady making announcements. I heard an exasperated sound coming from my nostrils while struggling between taller, broad-shouldered people. The smell of my own sweat was suffocating. Finally, I emerged from the crowd panting almost like a dog. There at the edge of the platform, I found Seema. I made my final steps toward her. The bag in my hand was getting heavier and heavier with every step.

"I thought I would have to leave without the bag!" she exclaimed jokingly. I went inside the car after her and found it was half-empty. With the new regulations, passengers had to sit leaving one seat between them vacant. So, they marked those seats with a red cross. I felt bad looking at this bloody-looking, obscene sign. The train gave a loud signal of departure.

"I must go," I said.

"I'll call you when I am in Bangalore," she replied. "I don't know when that will be. It's already too late." I exhaled from the bottom of my heavy heart. She was finally leaving and was happy to go. I gave her a goodbye kiss on her cheek.

As I stepped out of the train, it began to move. For a moment I thought I was drifting backward with the platform, but I realized that was an illusion as soon as I looked away from the train to the faint sun above. Seema came to the window to wave at me, smiling from ear to ear. I waved back, but failed to return the smile. It was strange. Up to this time, from the moment we left home, while driving and struggling with the crowd, I had waited for something really painful to occur right in the center of my chest, or at least at this very moment when the train was leaving, but to my shock, nothing really happened. Even before she was out of sight I turned and began to walk out of the station.

The glow of the sun on my skin as well as the brown tiles of the platform was soothing to my eyes. It was seeping out all sorts of coldness. I stopped to look through the panel of the waiting room. It was full of passengers, strolling here and there, worried about their baggage. At the other door, a crabby old man was sweeping the floor each time someone stepped onto it with dirty shoes. On the right, a mother was trying to breastfeed her crying child. There was a man on the same bench where I had been sitting. He was alone and held his head in between his palms. My eyes were glued to what was going on in the waiting room. It was hard to believe we were there just a few minutes ago, as if it was all a dream. Now, I felt I was woken up by a hard push or a blinding light or a deafening sound like a train siren.

A stout man went past me, shoving my shoulder. I stumbled, almost fell to the ground. Steadying myself, I walked on, my eyes on the floor until I was out of the automatic door. I was desperate to get away, far, far away from all the stone-faced people and the hubbub of the station.

                    * * *

On my way back home, I bought a pack of cigarettes. An unusual craving for something serious had been boiling up in me ever since I left the station, not to mention it had been several months since I had smoked.

I drove smoking and staring at the road stretching ahead. I had driven this way many times in my life, knowing it was the same road with the same billboards, the buildings on both sides, and the empty parks and shops. Knowing only that Seema and Jakie were not with me, I felt an emptiness coming back to me. I watched the fog slowly lifting. One could make out the upper windows of the tall buildings and clearly read the signposts on every corner, which were helpful if you were new in the city. The sun, parting through the leaves of trees that grew on the sides, was much clearer now.

I slowed down where I had seen the puppy that morning. My eyes searched the road and footpath and beyond, but found nothing. My heart was relieved when I saw no sign of a casualty. Hoping that the pup would be happy somewhere playing with its own shadow, I just moved on.

                    * * *

I knew Jakie would turn up in the window at any moment, hearing the sound of the car while I parked. I was accustomed to this behavior of his, but this time he didn't. This surprised me. I unlocked the door and walked into the house. My eyes looked instinctively for Jakie, but he was nowhere to be seen. What I saw instead was disturbing.

All the things that were once safe and undisturbed were scattered around the room. These included: the diary recording household expenditures, the bills for water and electricity, receipts of car loan installments, newspaper cuttings of advertisements of properties, the copies of CVs that I intended to mail to IT companies hopefully by the end of this month or the next, I hadn't decided which, and other important papers such as the medical report from a gastroenterologist who had rather frankly asked me if I was getting enough sleep or not. Next to these were cushions, a tablecloth, dog food, the hiking shoes we bought for a future adventure, and the woolen gloves that had been a gift to Seema which she had intentionally left behind on the couch as it was warmer where she was going, all were either torn or chewed up and scattered about the floor. It looked like the remnants left after a flood had ravaged a once-tidy house.

I would have to pick it all up either now or later. I chose later. First I wanted to see where Jakie was, and if he was all right. I found him cowering in a corner beside the couch, trying to make himself so compact that he'd not be seen. Almost hidden, he looked as though he were a different dog. To my shock, he didn't get up to greet me, nor did his tail even twitch. He moved only his eyes, which followed my feet as I proceeded toward him, looking at what he had done to the house.

I put my hand on his head. He shuddered away, as if unfamiliar with my touch. For a moment, anger rose in me, but I suppressed it. Sitting on the couch and staring at the chaos was simpler. Looking pitifully at Jakie, who in his curled-up position seemed sick, I puffed a cigarette. Then I got up, sauntered across the house, and looked at my reflection in the mirror over the sink while washing my hands and face. I thought of having a cup of coffee while watching TV. It was a stupid idea, I realized, looking at the condition of the house. My eyes fell upon the only photograph of my mother hanging on the wall above the couch. The dust made it look old and unclear. Then, I decided to take a nap.

Standing in the doorway, I looked at the quietness of the room; at the slow movement of the clock; the light pink stillness of the bedsheet, and then finally outside the window at the dying myrtle tree. I sat down on the bed heavily. The surface felt warm, as the sun had been there all the time I was out of the house, but I knew how cold it was underneath. I caressed the bedsheet and I closed my eyes. That's how the process of forgetting begins.

Jakie came into the room himself, walking limply, considering my face for a moment as if I were an intruder. His questioning eyes were somehow penetrating mine. Then he rubbed his left ear on my knee as if he finally recognized me.

"Oh, poor Jakie!" I patted him and let go of myself. I collapsed onto the bed.

Jakie came up on the bed, sniffed my nose and mouth, and sat down, carefully placing his muzzle on my chest. I let my fingers run through the fur below his ears, where he liked it the most. He moved closer, cuddling. We began to warm each other. I shut my eyes tight, then opened them and stared at the ceiling and the fan, until it all blurred and hot fluid came down my cheeks.

"It's too much," I said, "We've got to get out of this, Jakie. It's too fucking much."

Midnight Murder

They sat down at a square-cut table late at night in the bar.

"Do you trust me now?" Porush asked as he put his arm around his wife's neck.

"Yes, I do," Chetna replied, even though she had caught her husband's lustful eyes staring across at her friend Maya's breasts. It made her feel weak in her gut and bitter in her heart, but she chose to remain silent. It wasn't the right moment and she knew this situation was going to end tonight.

"Thanks, Maya, for bringing us here," said Porush. "And for clearing up all her doubts."

"I think it's my duty, isn't it?" Maya said, looking at Chetna.

Chetna meekly smiled at her, at them.

"We're best friends for life," said Maya, holding Chetna's hand.

"No, you are not!" Porush exclaimed. "Now, we are a family."

"Then I am glad to be a part of it," Maya winked at him.

Porush looked at his Rolex watch. It was slightly past 12 o'clock and the bar was already empty, which was strange in this part of the city that was used to staying awake throughout the night.

A tall, lean waiter came to take their orders. Instead of greeting or welcoming them, he looked at the three of them suspiciously. Chetna felt his stinging eyes on her neck and hastily hid her diamond necklace with her hand. Porush had given it to her on their recent wedding anniversary, three months ago. Despite this expensive present, the day still wasn't remembered as a good day in their married life.

"You'll take what, sir?" the waiter asked, not so politely.

"Beer!" Porush replied.

"I know what Chetna would like: red wine," Maya said.

"Sure," Chetna answered, trying not to look at the waiter.

"And you, Maya?" asked Porush. "Beer or wine?"

"Ummm... I like both," Maya replied, winking at Porush while squeezing Chetna's hand under the table. This made both of them a little uncomfortable in front of the waiter. Chetna looked away and Porush adjusted his expensive overcoat.

"This is the cleanest bar in the city, with the best service, and always smells good," Porush said, but the waiter, not being grateful for his kind words, awkwardly smirked at him. "Anyway, where's the washroom?" asked Porush.

The waiter led him to the washroom. They walked as if both were in a hurry.

"Is he really a waiter?" Chetna asked Maya in a muffled voice as she leaned from her chair when the two were out of her sight. Even though there was no one around to hear them talking, she spoke softly. "Or, is he the one you hired for... for what we are supposed to do tonight?"

"You guessed it right, my love," Maya replied. "You never go wrong with your intuitions."

"Can he really do it?" Chetna asked doubtfully. The waiter looked gaunt, weak, and weird when he walked.

"He's a professional."

"But he doesn't look like one," Chetna objected. "What if he opens his mouth later?"

"I paid him well."

"For more money, everybody does," Chetna countered.

"Not this one!" Maya smirked at Chetna's innocence while removing hair from her left ear. "I know men well. And being a woman, you must know men too. You can make them do whatever you want, if you know how."

"Oh, Maya. I'd never imagined this day would ever have come into our lives. Things could have been so different. No man should ever have done such a thing to me." Chetna shook her head and lowered her eyes in disappointment.

"Oh, my love!" Maya exclaimed. "What do you need a man for? I'm glad this day has come." Maya placed her hand on Chetna's naked thigh and rubbed. "Just don't be afraid tonight."

Chetna exhaled heavily, took a sip of water, and put the glass down. A few moments later, she drank some more. She felt she was losing her mind already. It was a grave crime they were going to commit. She looked around. The clean, dark green walls in the dim light haunted her.

"Can't we do this in a few days?" Chetna asked in agony.

"No chance!" objected Maya. "It took me three months to organize everything."

"But I'm scared."

"No, you aren't scared. You are just nervous and upset, and you shouldn't be."

"But..."

"Look! You have to do it before he does it to you, and sooner or later he's going to do it anyway. He told me about it that night."

"What else did he tell you?"

"I've already told you everything."

"I know. I know. " Chetna closed her eyes and put her head down in her cupped hands as if she was about to collapse. "I know what he thinks of me. But it is also true that I used to love him. After doing this, I'll be guilty for the rest of my life."

"You think too much, dear. That's the problem. Your perve husband deserves more than this, doesn't he? It was you who asked me to start all this: meeting him and even sleeping with him at last. I did it all at your request. Now he's shown his hidden fangs. This is the day we've been waiting for. Everything happened on time. You can't change your mind at the last moment. Our desired life depends on it. It's now or never. I'm doing all this for you, my dear. Just don't you get upset."

"All right! How are we going to do it?" Chetna asked.

"After the first round of drinks. I want your husband to soften a little. He won't be able to speak a word after the drink, I promise. The waiter is going to do the rest of the work."

"I won't stay here." Chetna tried to swallow down her fear, but she failed. "I won't stay. No matter what he has done to me, I can't watch it."

"Look! If you leave, people will blame it on you." Maya caressed her thigh again lustfully. "Please, stay, for me."

"Okay!" Chetna sighed into her never-ending confusion. "I'll stay."

Porush walked out of the washroom and sat down with them. In a while, the weird-looking waiter came out of the swinging door of the kitchen. With a tray in his hands, he walked unsteadily. His hand trembled while he placed the mugs on the table one by one. At last, he put down a saucer containing slices of fresh fruit. Thank God! Maya kept Porush's eyes engaged with her playful red lips as she began to put on more lipstick, so he didn't notice the waiter's undue frustration. Chetna wiped away the drops of sweat from her forehead as soon as the waiter left.

Chetna looked at her lonely mug of red wine between two mugs of beer. She thoughtfully peered into her mug as the tiny white bubbles rose up to the red surface. Nervously taking hold of it, she raised it slowly. All three clinked their mugs together and cheered. Everyone began sipping what was offered to them according to... what was planned. Everything was planned out well, Chetna thought. Maya was a charmer.

As Chetna watched her husband drinking the infected beer, she felt as if that vicious poison was also going down into her own stomach. She felt it in her throat and in the lungs. It made her sick. She moved her gaze away and looked down at the table which began to rotate. Red wine after several months was all to blame, she thought. She raised her brows, shook her head, and put the glass down with a thud.

"What happened?" Porush asked her while drinking.

"Nothing. This is strong." Chetna kept on sipping her drink nervously and looked up at Maya for some courage. For now, Maya's glittery eyes were as comfortable as her soft fingers were in the bed, and she knew everything had been figured out and finally she was going to be happy forever.

After placing the mug on the table, she examined her husband. He now looked drunk and worried. His eyes had turned red.

"Are you having fun?" Porush asked Chetna. His words sounded faint as they traveled across the table. She looked at his big, blurred face.

"Yes dear!" she tried to say, but began coughing. Often, when she felt anxious and tried to drink something—even just a glass of water—it soon made her cough. *One more sip would relax my throat.*

But it grew unbearably terrible. She felt a lump in her throat, growing bigger and bigger. And an ever-increasing burden on her eyebrows started giving her an intense headache. She shook her head. She wanted to puke it out.

As soon as Chetna closed her eyes to wonder what had just happened, she fell to the floor and heard the loud thud of her chair landing beside her. She couldn't scream. After a little bloating down in her stomach, something foamy gushed out of her mouth and she lay still. Maya and Porush considered her with a hint of a smile of satisfaction on their lips. The waiter who served them watched all this from a distance.

Back to Darkness

They stopped outside a twenty-seven-story five-star hotel. The building was gleaming as streetlights and headlights of passing cars reflected off its window glass. Ravi, who had come to this part of the city for the very first time, had admired all the skyscrapers, but he liked this one best. With the pride he had lately acquired in belonging to the city, he considered his image in the huge entry door of the hotel before following his uncle to the left.

While walking down a ramp to an unmarked passageway behind his uncle, Ravi found that he was not entering the hotel, but a completely different place.

Down there, in the dark narrowness, was a collapsible gate, above which a small sign was hanging. In tiny glittering lights the name, "RANJAN-PALACE," was visible. But the way it was poorly made, in contrast to the hotel, indicated that this hidden place was not owned and run by the hotel's affluent management.

A middle-aged man with a stern face and gray beard, in a watchman's typical black uniform, slid the gate open for them. He gave a reluctant bow to his uncle and spat in the corner when they went past him. Ravi turned back and found the old man staring at him pitifully from under his thick gray eyebrows. They entered a hallway and came out in a space that was completely hidden from people passing by.

Blinding blue light from tiny hanging bulbs was disturbingly hard to Ravi's eyes as he walked in. He was afraid to move out of his uncle's shadow. His uncle, a thirty-nine-year-old, doomed silver trader who had recently divorced his wife, walked dominantly ahead of him and winked at a skinny waiter. The waiter, with a tray in his hand, smiled at him, his teeth glowing blue in the bright light. Until the waiter went over to a group of people, while carrying the tray on his shoulder, Ravi couldn't move his eyes from the clinking glasses on the tray, spilling out something bloody-looking.

The further they went into this place, the more scared Ravi became. It was filled with smoke and a bittersweet smell unfamiliar to him. His uncle told him the people were smoking weed and cocaine. He saw some girls sitting among the different groups of men and giggling. All of them were smoking and drinking. Absurd pop music was playing in the background.

Moving past the people, his uncle walked in a carefree manner to a corner where he seemed at ease. As they were walking, the tiny blue overhead bulbs turned red, changing so slowly that it was almost imperceptible to Ravi's eyes until it was done. Now, the blue shirts of all the waiters moving across the hall had turned red like the thing they were serving. The walls around them and the carpet under their shoes were red too.

"I like everything in red," his uncle said.

Ravi turned to him and saw that his uncle's fat nose looked terrifyingly reddish. Then he checked the skin of his own fist; it was red too!

"The most peaceful place in the world," his uncle stated when they reached the corner of the room. They stood under a spinning chandelier that was projecting coin-like tiny lights onto the red carpet. Ravi watched them circling while his uncle's laughter reverberated in the empty corner. His uncle smoothed his hands on his pants and sat down on the couch which was made for three but his stout physique left no space for anyone else to sit but Ravi. No one was approaching this corner.

Ravi's knees were touching each other, his elbows were placed on them. He was shivering slightly.

"None of your friends are going to spot you here, boy," his uncle said, placing his hand on Ravi's shoulders. "Don't worry! I know this place. I've been visiting here since I was your age." He winked at him. Ravi leaned a little backward trying to make himself comfortable but that didn't seem to work.

A waiter came and placed a water pitcher on the table.

"He's eighteen plus," said his uncle and laughed. "He looks younger though, doesn't he?" he continued, looking at Ravi's small, rounded face.

"Yes, sir," the waiter replied, not bothering to look at Ravi. "What would you like, sir?"

"Are you new here?"

"Yes, sir."

"And, you ask the same thing to everyone who wants a little peace and quiet?"

"Sorry to bother you with my question. We have a vast collection of drinks. What kind would you like?"

"That's how you drill our ears with your piercing voice? Now go to hell and send that one here. That small one."

"Sure, sir. I'm sorry," the waiter said as he left.

"Don't be a geek like him," his uncle said to Ravi as the waiter retreated.

"Yes, he behaved quite strangely," Ravi agreed.

"No, he behaved exactly how a waiter should behave and how they trained them to...but don't be that person ever."

"What do you mean, Uncle?"

"Be strong! When someone says: "GO-TO-HELL," punch them right in their face no matter how hard your knuckles hurt afterward, ha-ha. But their nose must be bleeding!"

"A small one for the beginner," Ravi's uncle said to the second waiter who came over. "And I'll take the same, but make it a little stronger," his uncle added, then made an odd growling sound, grinding his teeth while pronouncing *stronger*. The red lights began to turn pink. The waiter leaned towards them, smiling sheepishly. Although this waiter seemed a little disturbed by Ravi's presence next to his uncle, Ravi himself was more disturbed than anyone else in the entire place.

"How old are you really?" his uncle asked Ravi after the waiter had gone.

"Sixteen."

"Do you like this city? Is it better than your town?"

"Yes, Uncle." Ravi caught his uncle's eyes observing his shy, skinny hands on the side of the couch.

"What d'you like the most about this city? Certainly not the traffic." His uncle cackled and then continued, "No parking space and everyone owns a car."

"I like the buildings," Ravi said. "They're so tall, and... also the people, their clothes. They're different from the people in my town. The people here don't like to rest. And the cars... they are so fast too."

"And the girls here are faster than the cars. Ha-ha. You like girls?"

Ravi just stared down at the floor.

"Don't be shy. I'm not going to tell anyone about your secrets. Whatever happens here between us must remain between us."

"Sure, Uncle."

"Then, look up at me."

Ravi looked up and then down again.

"Tell me, d'you like some cute chicks from your school?"

Ravi nodded shyly.

"How does she look? Slim, tall, cute, or chubby?"

Ravi didn't answer.

"Does she look hot?"

Ravi promptly looked into his uncle's eyes. Then, he felt something peculiar about looking into them and lowered his eyes again.

After a minute of bizarre silence, the waiter came back with a tray and gracefully put a variety of glasses and dishes on the table one by one. Ravi saw it all with his eyes bulging out and shoved himself backward.

"Not today," Ravi's uncle said to the waiter, not looking at him. "Go." And he waved the waiter away. Ravi wondered if the waiter was asking for something, maybe a tip.

"Isn't it hot here?" Ravi's uncle asked after a minute.

"Yes."

"You can take off your jacket." His uncle slid out of his tightly-fit jacket and hung it on the back of the sofa, spreading out his legs to relax. Timidly Ravi unzipped his own jacket and put it beside him. All the while, his uncle's eagle eyes were checking him out, noticing each nervous movement of his teenage body. Ravi sat there hugging himself.

"Drink it," his uncle offered. "You'll feel better."

Ravi touched and pulled his fingers back.

"It's too cold."

"Every cold thing makes you feel warm afterward and every hot thing cools you down. Remember that." His uncle laughed and touched Ravi's neck. A sudden sensation crossed his entire body. "You're already hot, boy." He winked at him.

Ravi shifted his eyes to the table to take hold of the glass carefully, his hands trembling. Picking it up, he looked into its floating redness. He had always wanted this day to come, at least once in his life, but not like this, not with his uncle whom he had always considered a father figure since his own father's death. In his regretful nervousness, Ravi looked at his uncle who had gulped down the glass full and waited for him to do so. Ravi closed his eyes, leaned a bit forward, lowered his head, and tasted it. He immediately shook his head hard, trying to erase the taste and strange sensation that stuck on his tongue. His uncle swallowed another as if the bloody thing was made of honey.

"You won't like this now, but after a few shots, it'll become sweeter than the sweetest thing you remember," his uncle said and drank another glass full. His eyes were now pink while his forehead shone the pale blue of the light. "Boy, in this city you need to learn new things and you need to learn them fast."

Resentful, Ravi took another sip, though, it tasted gingery and a bit better than before.

"So, tell me about that girl. You like her body?"
Ravi looked at him sharply but said nothing.
"In love with her?"
"No."
"Good! A man should never love."

"W–why?"

"Love is not for the man. The man is made for different kinds of drinks. And there are thousands in this world." His uncle raised the glass, smiling crookedly, not showing his teeth this time.

"Don't you miss Aunty?" Ravi dared to say something after a while.

"Why should I? She ditched me for another man. Yeah, I'm telling the truth, now. This damn thing makes you spit all the truth." He put the glass down on the table hard. "I'm happy that I'm divorced. Free now. Look! I can do anything and there are a lot of things to do in this city." He winked again at Ravi. "Now we are both alike, boy, and there are a lot of new things we could try right here tonight."

Ravi, not answering, looked at the clock. It was nearing one-thirty. He hoped it would be a bit faster when his uncle placed the palm of his firm hand on his thigh.

"So, what were you saying about your fucking girlfriend?" His uncle's eyes were red, his hair parted to hang down on his forehead.

"I... I don't have any, Uncle."

"You're a liar, aren't you? Young girls would die for such a cute face like yours." His uncle touched Ravi's cheek and rubbed it with the harsh skin of the back of his hand. "They would want to rub their cheeks here, ha–ha." As his uncle inched closer, Ravi pushed himself backward. His uncle's hand was still on his thigh. He dared not remove it.

"When a girl does so, you must know what to do next. Do you know where you should touch a girl first?" He felt his uncle's hand inching upward on his thigh slowly. "You know what they hide in here?" Ravi shivered as his uncle's sturdy hand touched it and pulled his hand back, raising his brows, admiringly. "You've grown up, child, haven't you?"

Bewildered about what he should do, Ravi took hold of another glass and emptied it as fast as he could.

"After this night you won't be a boy. You are becoming a man now," his uncle announced and refilled the glass. "Drink it!" Ravi looked down at his big hand that caressed his thigh all over again.

"It's time to try my taste. Drink this one, boy." The uncle's voice rose.

Ravi took it and finished it. He felt his throat melt down with it and the uncle stared at him while he drank it.

"Yeah! Now it's time to try another thing. A brand-new thing."

Restless, his uncle called for the same waiter after he had finished the whole bottle. The waiter came with another bottle and looked at Ravi with envious eyes. Before leaving, the waiter swayed to Ravi's right side and stretched up on his toes to touch something hanging from the ceiling. He slid the navy blue curtain closed, covering them from all sides. With the fabric walls around them, it looked like a dark, rounded room, which was getting hotter and hotter with Ravi's uneasy breaths. He began to feel wet in his armpits at the same time he was shivering. He had some dark presentiments. As soon as Ravi sensed his uncle leaning over him, he backed off, desperately wanting to get rid of his shadow.

"So, you never touched a girl in your life?" His uncle looked at the creases on Ravi's forehead. Ravi wiped the sweat away. "Answer me, boy!"

"No," he said.

"You know how to touch a girl?"

"No."

"Open your shirt."

"What?"

"It's too hot. No? Come on, open it." This sounded like a command.

His uncle opened his own shirt first and then removed his belt. Even though Ravi felt something blocking his eyesight, he could see his uncle's hairy belly in pink lights, inflating. "Now it feels like home," declared his uncle as he picked up the whole bottle and guzzled it down. While pouring it into his mouth, he put his other sweaty arm around Ravi's shoulder, pulling him even closer. Ravi stared at his arm until his uncle put down the bottle on the table with a thud.

"Open your shirt, man. You are sweating like hell."

With his eyes low, Ravi touched the fabric of his shirt. His pink hands initially failed to find the buttons even though he could measure the distance between them with his eyes. With great struggle and a humming sound in the back of his head, Ravi finally opened all the buttons, one by one. He felt like falling asleep. Then, he felt his sweat all across his body abruptly freezing. Suddenly, he shuddered as his uncle placed his hand on his naked shoulder.

"Now drink it."

"No," Ravi said, "I must not, Uncle."

"Drink it!" His uncle pulled him closer. He could feel his warm breath on his shoulder and chest.

"I don't... want...Uncle, please," Ravi begged.

"Of course, you want it, boy. Don't be shy. I'm your friend now. Let me teach you everything about girls and their bodies. Don't be shy. Be the one who can survive in this city as I did for years," his uncle said, sucking at his lower lip. Ravi felt his uncle's fingers fondling his shoulder, then his nails scratching his chest and then, there, his uncle pinched hard. Ravi turned away.

"No, Uncle, please," Ravi said, trying to wake himself up.

"You must become a man, tonight," his uncle said as he held the glass in one hand and grabbed Ravi's head from behind with the other to force him to drink all of it. His deep voice sounded loud in the small space. Half the wine gushed out from Ravi's mouth and down on his bare chest, then he heard it dripping on the leather. Ravi tried to push his uncle's big, hairy hands back, but he couldn't. He choked and finally, with all his force, jerked his big hand away, throwing the glass on the floor.

The larger man growled and pushed his nephew back down on the sofa. Ravi, light-headed, felt like flying downward in a vortex. He saw the ugly square of his uncle's face floating and coming down closer to his belly. Ravi felt cold and numb in his entire body. He felt cold in the knees, and his skinny legs trembled. Though he felt very small against his uncle, he writhed hard under the great pressure. Tightly closing his eyes and clenching his teeth, Ravi managed to fold up his right knee and then they both wrestled. His smaller hands couldn't push his uncle away. Ravi slipped and rolled down from the sofa and fell onto the red-carpeted floor. His head hit hard against a table leg. He shook his head. He felt like waking up from a deep sleep.

His uncle struggled to stand up straight and limped towards him like a hungry zombie, but stumbled on the table. The half-filled bottle rolled down, pouring out the rest of the wine all over the carpet. His uncle stood up and strode toward him. Ravi heaved himself up at the right moment. As his uncle came closer, Ravi tried to drive him back with both his hands, though it only threw Ravi backward. Balancing on his drunken legs and trying to walk steadily, his uncle shook his head like a bull and roared, "You little scum!"

As the red lights turned blue, and his uncle came closer, Ravi lifted the bottle off the ground and smashed it right in the center of his uncle's heavy face. He saw something dark running down from his uncle's nose and upper lip. Ravi stepped closer for another strike, but his uncle, now afraid, fell backward and toppled over the table, landing on the floor. His evil eyes stared at nothing.

Panting, Ravi stared down at his bloodstained fist, then looked at his uncle, terrified. Ravi could see that he was still breathing, so he relaxed knowing he was not dead. Ravi put on his shirt and jacket, then opened the curtain slightly. No one was there except for the small waiter who was playing something on his phone and had earbuds plugged in. The waiter looked up at Ravi with a blank stare. For a moment, they stared at each other, but the waiter said nothing, lowered his eyes, stood up, and went away. It was not his business.

Ravi noticed that the lights went off as he came back. He sat there on the couch in the dark, beside his uncle lying motionless. He could have left, but he chose not to, and waited there for more than two hours.

His uncle finally woke up, baffled as he found himself in an unexpected position with his nephew's eyes looking at his half-naked body. He stood up, then touched his nose with the tip of his fingers. It was still wet with his blood. He looked at Ravi again and then down at his shoes as though he wanted to bury himself. He was ashamed. Then, he started sobbing and kept sobbing while he put on his shirt and jacket and clasped the belt. After wiping his cheeks, he found Ravi still glaring at him. He lowered his eyes again in shame and sat down on the sofa beside Ravi.

"All because I miss her, Ravi," he cried loudly. "I utterly miss her every single day. I miss her!" His uncle choked as he spoke.

Ravi grabbed his shoulder and raised him up. It was difficult for his uncle to stand on his legs.

"I hate myself," he sobbed. "I'm going to kill myself someday, Ravi."

Ravi, not answering, walked him to the door and then outside. The watchman stood there, not sleepy, staring at both of them with his spiteful dark eyes under thick brows. As his uncle passed, he saw the bloodstains on his upper lip and nose. The watchman spat, then smiled proudly at Ravi. Ravi smiled back and kept smiling as he helped his uncle walk down the street.

Outside, it was dark and cool, and the road was empty except for two or three taxis. Ravi could take his uncle back to his house easily. He kept on walking straight while the darkness stretched ahead, not looking back at the tall dazzling building that he liked the most in this city. He didn't hate the building or the city, but he no longer felt he belonged to it. He didn't even want to think about it. While walking with the weight of his uncle's stout body, all he thought about was the first-morning train back to his hometown.

Dead River

A small stream that came out of the Himalayas' womb had become a fairly wide river. The green, sloping hills at the foot of the Himalayan range, with sharp, gray rocks and rounded, white boulders in the valleys, provided a channel quite rough and steep that helped the river carry its fierce flow. It ran alongside a winding road and below risky narrow bridges.

Sitting next to her father in a slowly moving public transport bus, Divya was peering out of the window, cherishing the vision of the white bubbly foam on the top of the roaring waves, with giant hills in the background. Her eyes were delighted with the sight, as she had never seen a river before in such a furious avatar.

"Dad, can we just go down to the river?" asked Divya. "Wouldn't it be cool to touch the water?"

"In the summer, it's not so cool. But we can't go there now," her father replied, not looking into her nine-year-old eyes, which gleamed with wonder.

But sitting in the same position for three hours had bored the little girl. Now, she couldn't resist the call of the river.

"When?" Her brows quickly turned desperate.

"As soon as we get off the bus," her father assured her.

"Really?" Divya jumped from her seat. "Thank you for bringing me here with you, Dad." She hugged her father's arm. "Could I also jump into the river and try to swim for a while?"

"No, you can't do it where we're going. It might be too deep in some places."

"Can we play in the water at the banks at least?" she asked, remembering an incident when her mother had carried her into a large pond with ducks floating around them and they had splashed the water onto each other until they were wet from hair to toe.

"No!" her father said. "You'll stay on the bank and I will walk into the river and immerse this in the water. It's a ritual. That's why we have come here. We are not here to play."

Divya's hopes were deflated. Then, she reflected, she could at least watch the water rushing by as it was doing here.

A handbag rested on her father's thigh. Inside was a small clay pot, wrapped in a red cotton cloth, tightly knotted at the top.

"Your mother's ashes are in this bag," her father said. "It's a ritual we are going to do, not play," he repeated.

"But why this river?" Divya asked. "We also have a river back in our town too."

"Because this river is sacred," he answered. "It's called a mother river in our holy scriptures. We will pour the ashes of your mother into its holy water. It's obligatory."

Divya turned gloomy and thought of the past when she spent most of her time around her mother. It had been two months since her mother died, yet every evening Divya imagined that her mother would be coming back any moment and asking Divya if she had finished all her homework. Sitting next to her father on the bus, she solemnly looked at the bag that consisted of all that her mother had left behind: her ashes.

After a while, as the bus took another sharp left turn into the hills, she couldn't see the river anymore, though the sound of rushing water was never far away. She knew it was there, out of sight, right behind the row of hills.

"Dad, what does 'sacred' mean?" Divya asked when, at the next turn of the road, the river came back into her sight.

"Things that we worship."

"Like the silver idol of Mother Goddess at our home?"

"Exactly!"

"Ah. This river really looks sacred. I would also love to worship this river." Divya's eyes showed the purity of childish desires. "Will Mamma come back to us after the ritual?"

"No. That's not possible." Her father rolled his tongue in his mouth.

"Why not? We worship Mother Goddess at our home, and we are here to worship mother river. Can't I ask for my mamma? Is mother river so angry at me because I don't do my homework nowadays?"

Her father, not looking at her, bit his lower lip thoughtfully. Each time Divya had asked about her mother, and when she was coming back to them, he kept his mouth shut, and his eyes became restless.

Divya became disheartened again because of her father's usual silence on the matter. She turned back to look out the window. This was better. It was soothing to see the river through the bushes and leaves of the trees that grew wildly along the road. Though it looked unstoppable earlier, the pace of the river had now slackened drastically. The whites of the waves had disappeared into the blue of the sky reflecting on the water. There were no more big rocks and boulders in the waterway, and the land was flatter here. Instead of bouncing riotously in a narrow channel like before, the river had become wider and was flowing slowly, even sluggishly. The burble, too, wasn't as loud as before. The river seemed like a girl who had turned into a mature woman, quiet and sensible.

"Dad, are we going to stop soon, or not?" She was impatient.

Just a short while later, the bus halted at a station with a small market and a huge crowd. As soon as they got off the bus, old women in the market began calling to the passengers to buy fruit, flower garlands, and toys, clumsily made of wood and clay. Divya thought she would ask her dad for a toy when they returned. Her father bought a garland and a few individual marigold flowers.

To the east, beyond the market, there was a tall, well-built, ancient temple made entirely of black rocks.

"We're going down there," her father pointed to the temple.

"Is the river in that direction?"

"Yes, right there behind the temple."

Divya proudly smiled at her accurate guess.

Wind from the east blew cool on them as they took off their shoes and advanced toward the temple. Divya was jumpy with excitement. The bare ground they walked on had been leveled evenly so anyone could reach the river without hurting their bare feet. To show respect, no one wore shoes in this sacred space. Divya followed her father, staring down at the footprints imprinted in the damp ground.

The low rustling of the river was calling, as though she was as impatient to meet Divya as Divya was to meet her.

They first bowed to the main deity in the ebony temple. Outside were four sages wearing saffron robes, sitting solitary in mossy, damp spots in the shade of a banyan tree. Divya noticed that the entire shrine area was full of gigantic banyan trees. Their leaves were rustling, and their branches were swiftly moving in the early afternoon breeze. Everything at the shrine was under their cool shadow, except the river. The river looked glittering bright with perpendicular sunlight reflecting in it.

"Dad, aren't we going there?" Divya pointed to the river.

"We are," her father answered. "But, would you like to eat roasted corn first?" he asked.

"Yes, Dad. I'm so very hungry." It had been a four-hour-long ride from their town to the shrine. They had only had a light tasteless breakfast her father made at home before they departed.

Her father bought her corn from an old lady who was turning and twisting ears of corn on live coals in the corner of the courtyard opposite the temple. The roasted corn was hot, crispy, and sour, the lady had smeared lemon juice all over it before handing it to them still covered in its own corn husk. Divya liked its sweet, white juiciness that burst in her mouth as soon as she bit her teeth into the corn. They ate while they walked. She had finished savoring it by the time they reached the river.

At the river there were more people than she expected; many were sitting on the bank of the river, their legs relaxing in the water, and many others were swimming from one side of the river to the other. And, you could hear them splashing in the water. To the left, there was a big gray wall built across the river.

"Dad, what is that thing?" Divya asked, frowning as she pointed to it.

"That's called a dam."

"What's a dam?"

"It stops the water."

"Why?"

"So, that we can get more water from the river to drink."

"But why can't we let the river flow freely? It has so much water without the dam; it makes the river look ugly."

Again, her questions went unanswered. As they went further towards where people were sitting, she found heaps of garbage right on the edge of the river. There were plastic bottles, polythene bags, abandoned clothes, baby shoes, rotten coconuts, dead flowers, and a lot of other trash. All these things were floating in the dull green water at the shore, and yes, some corn husks too. At that moment, Divya was dismayed that the river wasn't the same anymore. This was not the river she had admired from the window of the bus. Neither the flow nor the sound of it was the same. It had suddenly become old and lifeless. When she had seen the river from the bus, she had wanted to jump into its crystal-clear water, however, here, now, it had turned into a dull green river. In some places, where the water wasn't flowing, it was much darker than that.

"This is not the same river, Dad," she said, looking at the dirty water, which the push of the current brought toward her. She backed away to protect her toes.

"This is the same river, Divya," he said.

"But it doesn't look the same," Divya objected. "And, you promised to take me out to that river, the real river, the other river." Divya jerked her hand in frustration and threw away the corn husk into the water where the garbage was floating.

"Divya!" shouted the father. "Pick it up now. It's bad manners."

"But why?"

"It is a sacred river."

"But it's a very very very dirty river already."

"Don't talk to me like this, and pick that up quickly."

Reluctantly, Divya stepped into the dirty water and picked up the corn husk with her hand, then threw it away in a broken dustbin nearby. She then submissively followed her father.

A priest, who was bald except for a long pigtail that touched the back of his neck, walked toward them. He greeted them, holding both of his hands together in front of his chest. Her father greeted him in the same manner. Her father and the priest talked for a while, almost whispering to each other, then the priest took them both into the roofless temple built at the shore.

There, they sat down in front of an old idol of a deity. Divya sat down next to her father and looked at the river angrily and thoughtfully. The bald priest closed his eyes and muttered something to himself, his torso swaying back and forth matching the rhythm of his *mantras*. Then, after offering a handful of rice to the disfigured deity in front of them, he started telling a story of the great heavenly river, which was flowing right in front of them. He said that the river is of great significance in our culture. Smiling proudly and showing his little crooked, yellowed teeth to Divya, he told her about the miraculous nature of its holy water, that it can even cure some incurable skin diseases. But Divya only looked at the clusters of plastic waste, garbage, and corn husks that floated on the water.

How could it have changed so drastically? It is not the same river. Divya looked at the river. She could not listen to the words of the priest; the change of the river bothered her so much. But she knew she was wrong in thinking it was a different river, as she herself had observed it from the bus. The only difference was that there were no people around the river earlier, and here it was surrounded by a great number of devotees. Or, maybe it was the dam that prevented its water from flowing freely and this was the reason behind its horrible transformation.

After some time, both her father and the priest stood up and waded into the river as far as they could without swimming. The greenish water touched her father's waist, then he dipped down into it, and came up headfirst. Water poured down, flattening his hair. He walked out, toward her, the beads of polluted water dripping off his clothes. As he sat down in his soaked clothes beside her, Divya couldn't resist moving away from him.

She loved her dad a lot, but one time, Divya couldn't love her dad. That day he had torn the books Mamma was reading and slapped her, saying she shouldn't waste all her time reading them while there was nothing to eat in the kitchen. Mamma had fallen down helplessly. Her *sari* had come unhooked from her shoulder and her hair was spread out on the floor. There was blood on her lips, too, when she sat up again. That day, for the first time, Mamma looked very ugly and helpless, just like this poor river in front of her now. On that day Divya couldn't love her dad. The whole day she was just afraid of him.

After some time, the priest and her father went back to the river with the covered pot, the coconut the priest used for worshiping, the garland of flowers they bought earlier, and some loose flowers. Divya got up to follow her father, but he told her to stay right there, out of the water.

Divya immediately thought back to the last time her father commanded her to stop where she was, exactly the same way. It was when Mamma shrieked from her bedroom, and her father, with a horrific and bewildered look on his face, dashed into the room to see what had happened to her mamma. This incident took place the morning after they had argued the whole night, keeping Divya from sleep. She stood there at the doorway when she saw her mamma lying on the floor lifelessly. All the strength in Divya's legs vanished and she also fell to the floor. She lost consciousness and had no idea what happened after that. Later, she was told that her mamma would no longer live with them.

Now, standing on the shore, her feet were frozen, her mind taking the ride back and forth in memories. A wave of tainted water touched her toes, but she didn't retreat this time. Instead, she saw her father and the priest pouring the silvery ashes into the listlessly moving water. The ashes only made the water look darker and dirtier.

When her father came back to her after touching the priest's feet, she didn't talk to him, even when they walked out of the shrine. For half an hour they waited at the bus stop and the wind hissed in her ears. Although Divya closely observed the joyous children her own age buying toys from the stalls, she asked nothing for herself. She didn't want a toy now. Her father asked if she was okay. She only nodded.

A public transport bus came, halted in front of them and they got on. It was headed in the direction of their home. Divya sat at the window seat, and all along the way, she stared at the river, hiding her miserable face from her dad. As the bus went on, she noticed the water of the river turned clean again and it was roaring fiercely as if nothing would stop it ever, which she knew was utterly wrong. All of a sudden, from just looking at the river, she burst into tears and began to sob loudly.

"What's the matter, Divya?" her father asked, putting his arm around her. "Are you missing your mamma?"

She stopped sobbing and gulped down her tears.

"You, too, polluted the river like everyone else," she blurted out and turned her red face towards the window.

"What I did was a ritual for your mamma," her father answered. "She must be happy now."

"No, she isn't. She can't be happy polluting a river."

"Look, it was an obligatory ritual. Everyone in our religion has to do it. It's not like throwing a corn husk into the water. These two acts are not the same."

"But you made the water dirty too. What's the difference?"

"We were not making it dirty. It is one of the ways to worship the Mother Goddess."

"Then we shouldn't worship anything at all," Divya said and refused to say anything more on their journey back to their town.

The Curtain and the Clouds

"Look at the clouds."

"Clouds? Really?"

"Yes, there they are."

"Are you sure?" Rahul asked.

"Why can't you trust me?" his wife asked, anxiously.

"I do trust you."

"You never like anything I like," complained Teena hopelessly.

It was one of the cold mornings of January, the month that marked the five years of their marriage. It was also the tenth month of the lockdown due to the COVID–19 pandemic, so they had no business outside, nor inside, and they were running out of money as well as their interest in almost everything.

Seated on the couch, they had sipped their coffee together and had not talked to each other. Teena stood up and went to the window to look at the clouds, but Rahul disappointed her all over again with his apathy. He raised his brows and stood up grudgingly. Without uttering anything, he strode straight to the window where Teena was. She held the dark blue curtain slightly above her right shoulder, now, not waiting for him anymore to come over, and her smile had gone somewhere.

Standing there, Rahul felt Teena's eyes on the side of his neck. He turned to her, and, when their eyes met, she dropped her head and looked at the floor thoughtfully, her fist still squeezing the curtain. Before her husband could say anything about the clouds, the sky or the whole scene out there, the curtain fell from her hand abruptly and there were no more clouds, only an expanse of navy blue silk stretching wide across his face.

Teena stepped back and sat again on the couch, hugging herself. She buried her head in her arms and stared at the whiteness of the tiled floor. She lifted her face and in front of her eyes, on the table, was the half-filled coffee mug Rahul had left.

The mug had been warm in Rahul's palms and he had liked holding it, but he realized it would now be cold—cold and alone. Rahul wouldn't drink that coffee for sure, but he felt bad thinking about it. This feeling would ruin his day, his writing, and the stories he was working on. So, he made up his mind and raised the curtain slowly as though it was made of lead.

"Yes, you are right. The clouds look beautiful," he declared.

"I don't care," Teena replied from behind him, her head down.

Without letting the curtain fall, he turned back and considered the whole of her at once. In such a sullen posture she looked so small.

"I thought you liked them," Rahul said.

"Yes, I did but you don't."

"I just said the clouds are beautiful, didn't you hear that?"

"But you don't mean it."

"How can you say that?" Rahul pretended to be stunned for he knew that she was right.

"I know it," Teena replied.

"That's the matter with you, always."

"Don't talk to me like this."

"I am talking fine," he objected. "I'm fine."

He tried to smile, but Teena was still not moving or caring to answer him. Suddenly he no longer felt fine. There was a time when Rahul admired everything his wife adored, whether it was the coffee shop with old, Greek-styled furniture at the corner of the street in the old city, the traditional Indian print of cushions, the new trend of graying the men's hair, or a teenage movie about a road trip into the wilderness. Teena had an adventurous soul and Rahul loved it. Although he had never engaged in any of her risky pursuits such as rock climbing or cliff jumping, when she always lacked his company, he had lauded her for what she was made of, for her spirit of an adrenaline junkie.

But, in just one day, everything changed. The sky had filled with clouds and lightning, and the entire city had been flooded by evening. That day, despite the enormous pressure of meeting deadlines for submitting articles to the magazines where he worked, Rahul preferred to stay at home, but not Teena. Until the morning of that day, she had always kissed him goodbye before leaving. That day she wouldn't make eye contact with him when she finally returned home, all wet. He could see her brand-new blue undergarments through the sheer fabric of her *kurti*.

Rahul was told later that his wife could not make it to their apartment as normal because of the heavy downpour and the flooded streets. Rahul had been told this many times by different people, and he despised hearing it each time. A week before this, he had found sickly sweet morning messages from a colleague on her phone. They were the reasons behind all the bitterness between husband and wife. After that, Teena left her designing job, shut down the business she'd started only weeks before, and decided to be a housewife forever. But this only made things worse.

"Yes, that was the matter with you, always!" Rahul blurted out, remembering.

"Please," the wife said, closing her eyes. "Stop it."

"You started it."

They didn't talk for a while.

"Rahul!" She looked at him, her eyes now begging. "It's been too long."

"So what?"

"We must stop it. We can't go on like this. It's distressing. We could be fine together like we were before, couldn't we?"

"I don't think so," Rahul replied in an attempt to end the argument.

"Why?" Teena asked loudly. "I don't understand. Why can't we talk while drinking our morning coffee or eating supper like we used to? Why can't you hug me from behind and say that I look beautiful when I brush my hair in front of the dresser? Why do we have to behave as though the other one doesn't exist anymore? Why can't you trust me even when I say there are clouds out there?"

While she spoke, Rahul remained silent, rolled his tongue and examined the ceiling which looked unfamiliar to him with its worn-out textures.

"I don't know," he said when she was finished.

"It's been three years," said Teena, "and I've done everything I could do to gain your trust back."

"You cannot fix it." Rahul considered her blankly as he solemnly replied.

Teena swallowed in disappointment. Rahul glanced at her hands and saw her frenzied fingers moving into the gaps of one another, her toes were pressing on the floor. Even sitting like this, she was beautiful. He had loved her. Rahul always loved her. Standing there at the window and looking at her hair and the pink edge of her left ear, he wanted to love her. But the change Rahul went through was painful and came very strong when it came. This was visible in the way he talked, in the way he wrote, and in the way he remained silent. Each time he had shown his love to her, he believed, it only made him weaker. He was feeling weak even now, he couldn't move from this spot.

"We cannot go on like this. We have to sort it out one way or another." His wife stood up from the couch, sighed heavily, and trying not to look at him again, thrust her hands into the pockets of her overcoat.

"Okay then!" Her husband shrugged and turned to the window. His legs felt cold and feeble when he heard her shuffle across the hallway to her bedroom and slam the door shut. She always does this, he said to himself. He tried to stand still and firm, gazing out the window. Yes, clouds over the pine trees were moving beautifully, going back to the Arabian Sea where they had come from a few months ago. They were darker then and had rained all over the country. The monsoon was over. The sky was now filled with retreating clouds. Rahul would have liked the sky more if it was clear and blue and spotless like it was that last morning before the monsoon.

He had always loved clear things—clear and simple. That's how he wanted to write. And, in such plain weather, you could also slide the window glass open and feel the warmth of the sun hitting your face, melting down your winter-tightened muscles. Everyone must like the sun and no one should have said that the clouds are beautiful on such a damn morning of a cruel month. The clouds filled the sky needlessly, he thought.

He looked down at the floor as he heard a low sobbing coming from her bedroom. *She always does this*, he said to himself, hatefully. He stared at the gray laminated wood and the cold, golden knob of the closed door, and his hand, still holding the curtain, was now rock-frozen. He had ruined the day and wouldn't be able to write anything at all, it cannot be changed now. It's out of his hands. And he was too weak to stand there. It was bad all over again.

"Are you okay?" he said out loud.

"Please shut up, Rahul, please," Teena shrieked in a not-so-womanly voice that echoed from the bedroom. "I beg you. Please!"

Maybe I should have said the clouds are really beautiful, even when I feel they are not, Rahul thought as he looked ruefully back at the half-filled coffee mug left at the table. Closing his eyes tighter than ever, Rahul shook his head. He let the curtain fall. Now, he needed a little wine, not coffee, maybe some cigarettes too, that would be fine. He knew the day was already ruined.

In Search of the Lambs

Almost all the villagers had gone. I saw the last of them crossing the narrow wooden bridge with bags on their shoulders. They gathered around where we had blocked the only road into the valley before dawn. Beyond the sloping farms, and a half-frozen stream that cut through the snow-layered pastures, stood an army truck at the edge of the road. A few soldiers helped old people climb into the truck, and thrust in their belongings. Then, that overloaded truck had gone, leaving the rest of the people to wait and hope. After a while, another truck came, and the people rushed into it impatiently. As soon as this truck too disappeared in the expanding shadows of the southern mountains, the first one had returned, bringing a hint of a smile on the winter-beaten faces of the rest of the people who had been waiting.

This cycle had been running nonstop for eleven hours in front of our eyes at the foothills of the northwestern valley of Kashmir. After we had vacated three villages in the valley, we were informed of the terror attack that occurred here last night. A big failure of intelligence, according to news reports. We received orders immediately that the village should have been cleared out in a single day. So, we started off early since this village was located deep in the valley.

Being a newly appointed commanding officer of the patrolling unit, I had to keep an eye on every movement until all the villagers had been safely transported elsewhere. That was all.

However, in the bone-shattering winter at the beginning of January, even standing still wasn't an easy task. All day, the sun had been showering its solace over us, but it was now exhausted and wanted to rest behind the white mountains. With rifles in our hands, we were no more than statues carved out of the Himalayan rocks with some snowflakes resting on our shoulders and now we, too, were exhausted.

After the truck had gone with all the rest of the people, I smiled proudly at one of the officers standing by me. We had completed the long and arduous task without the loss of a single life. I felt an incredible sense of relief when I saw that there were no more villagers waiting to go. Then, I and the three remaining soldiers were commanded to go back to the deserted village for the final probe.

Keeping the bayonet of the INSAS rifle in front of my chin, I crawled in a low ready position along a stone wall. In many dark places in the village, there might have been bombs hidden underneath the ground, and possibly a few armed adults could be lurking here and there as well. These days it has become normal for this region's young adults to conspire with terrorist organizations and act out with double standards.

Slowly and carefully, we kept on moving further, beyond the stream and up the hill. The higher we went, the darker it became. The snowy wind now started to grasp our throats. The village looked as if it had lost its soul. Old and dull, the houses, with cracked clay walls, were forced to abandon their former togetherness. I felt something breaking inside of me when I heard dry leaves rasping on the harsh ground and the wooden doors of the empty houses swinging back and forth with the wind, exposing the cold and dead interior walls. Villagers had to leave behind their goats and hens, which were bleating and clucking at the creak of our shoes as if trying to wake up the dead.

We searched half the village, looked behind every rock and wall, then we finally came to the ravaged part of the village where the blast had taken place last night. On the hilltop was an old seminary painted dark green, where they threw the bomb. Although only a wreck now, on the collapsed walls I could see some *Arabic* letters. Much about the god was written on these broken walls, and to be true, we were scared as hell as we walked on the debris. We turned the rubble and shook up each body we found down there. Their mixed-up blood had dried into stains. They said that a hundred villagers were killed, but more bodies might have been buried deep under the holy debris.

By walking on, we reached the last stone wall of the village which must have failed to guard it. Downhill, on the other side too were a few shacks.

"Let's go down there," I told my men, trying not to look back.

Looking through the rifle scope, I found an old man in a silvery-grey phiran, sitting against the wall of a shack, peering at the purple sky. He seemed to be talking with someone. Although he was too old to be any danger to us, we had to cluster around him. Deciding to go to him separately, I sent a soldier to the right, and two to the left, while I moved straight forward.

The old man remained oblivious to our approach until the tip of my gun touched his throat. He opened his tired eyes and smiled at me. His face, covered with old chickenpox marks, looked red and terrible. I indicated to the soldiers to search in and around the cottage. They went and came back to me, indicating all was clear.

"Who are you?" I asked the old man.

"You are in my house, tell me who you are?"

"You know who I am, can't you see this?"

"No," the old man said, "I can't see anything in the dark."

"It's not fully dark yet, but it will be soon. Are you a villager?"

"I was an Imam here."

"Many died in the seminary last night, I wonder, how did an Imam survive?"

He held his old dusty hands up in the air while my companions searched in deep pockets of his phiran and his underclothes. The grip of my finger tightened on the trigger as I pushed myself ahead.

"I was out of the seminary," he said when the soldiers were done. "I was looking for my lambs."

"Your lambs must be lucky for you. But you should be gone from here by now. The trucks are transporting your people down to the army camp. Why were you not with them, the other villagers?"

"I have been waiting," he said thoughtfully.

"For?"

"The sun's down and my lambs have not returned yet."

"Do they always come back on time?"

"Yes, they do!" His eyes staring at the sky seemed confident.

"If you know which direction your lambs have gone, you can find them later."

"I don't know," he said, looking in the west. "Somehow they broke the chains and ran away right before it happened. Animals sometimes have presentiments, but they do know the way back. They will be here and find no one if I have left with you. This will scare them away. I cannot leave with you. I must stay. I must wait."

The old, light brown eyes looked into mine as the cool wind crossed us. My eyes fell onto the gray sight beyond the hills; the mountains looked massive, and their edges were sharp and silvery against the moon behind them. With its beauty and horror, the dreamy-looking northern country was, in many ways, very different from the rest of the nation. You never want to look into the northwest to search for any beauty as it always makes you feel cold in your legs. So, you learn to look at it only with the burning anger in your eyes.

"They better not come here," I said to the old man, not looking down at him. "There is nothing left for them. Try to get up now. We'll take you down there. It's almost dark and you cannot see in the dark, right?"

"But they can see in the dark. I raised them here. They cannot forget the way to their home. But I am afraid..."

"Of what?"

"What if they have gone to the other side? They have never been taught to recognize the difference."

"Oh, then I must say, either your lambs have been killed, or if not they are fine, and they'll come back here."

"Then, can I really come here to find them later?" he asked. "Can you promise me?"

I dared not say anything. It wasn't a good place or a good time to talk about the lost lambs.

"Listen!" I said instead. "If you don't get up, we'll have to carry you."

The old man laughed and shook his head sluggishly. He tried to get up. The soldiers helped him to stand fully, but the long wait for the lambs had made his knees weak. He trembled and fell to the ground.

I handed my gun to one of my companions. Then, wrapping my arm around his stiff old back, I lifted him up over my shoulder, and we began to walk down the hill. My companions, with rifles ready to shoot, guarded us on all sides until we had crossed and left the wooden bridge behind.

A truck was waiting for us, and in the beams of its headlights, a tall, Sikh soldier was waving both his big hands towards us. The sight of him warmed us enough to cover the remaining distance; I was desperate to go back to our camp. Our duty was done, we had found what we were looking for, but the eyes of the old man on my shoulder were still looking back at the village, in search of the lambs.

Acknowledgments

My father wrote a poem when I was born. I wasn't fortunate enough to meet my grandfather, but I grew up reading the poems he wrote in a diary, a true treasure he had left behind for us. So it is quite natural that I always aspired to be a writer, to carry on their legacy.

I have dedicated this book to the person who came into my life as a blessing at such a time when I needed it the most: my lovely daughter, Jenisha. I also thank my father for introducing me to the strength of the English language at quite an early age, and my mother for keeping track of my character. Many thanks to my wife, Supriya, for accompanying me on this journey while tolerating my mood swings.

It was such an honor to work with Marie Manthe, the founder of Lighted Lake Press, who believed in these stories and turned my dream into a reality, making this book possible. I tried my best to weave whatever I learned about life, people, their thoughts, their way of loving (or hating), the relationships they like to carry or decide to dump, the rituals they believe in, the national issues that affect them personally, and many other things into the cohesive stories. I hope some of them will become your favorite ones.

I am also grateful to the journals, magazines, and anthologies where earlier versions of these stories first appeared: *Novus Literary Journal*, *Forever Endeavour*, *Star Gazette Magazine*, *Radiate Literary Journal*, *Together Magazine*, *March Journal*, *The Firefly Review*, *Yawp*, *ARC Journal*, *Flare Journal*, *The Notions of Living*, *The Notions of Healing*, and others.

About the Author

Divyank J. writes stories about animals, mountains, and broken people on their journey to healing. He dives into the psyche of his characters while narrating their mundane, everyday human experiences. Growing up as a child in Ogna, a town near Udaipur, he always admired the beauty of nature, a simple lifestyle, and solo traveling, and his writing also reflects this. Some of his stories fortunately found a deserving place in various national and international magazines, journals, and anthologies. Currently, he resides in Udaipur, Rajasthan, India with his family. In 2022 he earned his master's in English literature and started a quarterly literary arts journal, *The Hemlock*. Apart from writing, he teaches accountancy to young students, draws pencil sketches, spends time with his daughter, and on weekends often goes out on trips with his dog.